SIX-GUN NEMESIS

In Chaparral Bend a gallows is being raised for youngster Ty Garland, accused of bank robbery. But his old ma claims he is innocent. Hollis Kitchenbrand is inclined to believe her, especially as notorious gunman Angel Addison and his gang seem to be involved. Kitchenbrand's search for answers leads him to the outlaw roost of Addisonville. He can count on the support of the old woman and a girl he has rescued, but will that be enough to succeed against overwhelming odds?

COLIN BAINBRIDGE

◆

SIX-GUN NEMESIS

Complete and Unabridged

LINFORD
Leicester

First published in Great Britain in 2012 by
Robert Hale Limited
London

First Linford Edition
published 2014
by arrangement with
Robert Hale Limited
London

*A catalogue record for this book is available
from the British Library.*

ISBN 978–1–4448–1920–5

Published by
F. A. Thorpe (Publishing)
Anstey, Leicestershire

Set by Words & Graphics Ltd.
Anstey, Leicestershire
Printed and bound in Great Britain by
T. J. International Ltd., Padstow, Cornwall

This book is printed on acid-free paper

1

Kitchenbrand drew the roan to a halt and reached for his field glasses. Something strange had caught his eye. At first he had ignored it but, whatever it was, it kept popping in and out of his field of vision. It seemed to be some giant bird. It would appear for a moment and then vanish in the long grass, behind some bushes or a rock. The moments extended as he sat his horse and he was about to conclude that he must have been mistaken when he saw the object again. He clapped the glasses to his eyes and succeeded in getting a fleeting glimpse of something distinctly odd, but he still couldn't make out what it was. Touching his spurs to the gelding's flanks, he turned off the trail, reaching for his rifle as he did so. After riding for a time he stopped again. He could see no sign of the strange object but he thought he could detect a faint murmuring sound. He strained his ears as it came again, subsiding to a low mumble. The sound seemed to issue from a patch of vegetation and as he approached cautiously he began to pick out distinct words and expletives:

'Landogoshen . . . Sassafras . . . Tarnation.'

If that's a bird, he pondered, *it ain't much of a song-bird.*

The voice was high-pitched as it emerged from its background droning. Kitchenbrand slid the rifle back into its scabbard and dismounted. He walked towards the bushes and pushed his way through. In a small clearing there lay what seemed to confirm his impression that he had detected some unknown species of bird till he perceived a human figure covered with feathers. As he got close he saw that it was an old woman, and at the same moment in which he recognized her, the woman sensed his presence. She looked up at him through eyes which seemed preternaturally sharp and blazing through the black substance which smeared the rest of her features.

'Consarnit, I ain't scared of you,' she hissed.

'You ain't got no cause to be scared, ma'am,' Kitchenbrand replied. He knelt down beside her.

'Don't, you go touchin' me,' she muttered. 'I ain't let no man touch me for thirty years and I don't intend no-one doin' it now.'

'Ma'am,' Kitchenbrand replied, 'it was the furthest thing from my mind.'

'I know your type,' she replied. 'Ain't no woman safe no matter how she's fixed.'

'Ma'am, I can see you ain't in the best of shapes. If you give me a moment, I have something which might help to restore you a little.' He turned away and walked back to his horse. *Tarred and feathered*, he thought, *but over her clothes*. Still, it was a bad thing to do to an old woman.

3

In a few moments he was back with a flask of whiskey and a canteen of water.

'Here, take a swig of this,' he said. She didn't offer any objections; sitting up straight, she poured a good draught of the liquor down her throat.

'I got a canteen of water,' Kitchenbrand said. 'Maybe you could start tidying yourself up some.' He passed her the canteen. She looked at him with her piercing eyes, then snatched it from his grasp. 'I could help remove some of those feathers,' he suggested.

'Like I said, you just keep your hands off of me,' she replied. 'Your kind are always lookin' for some excuse to start a-pawin' at female flesh.' She took another swig of the whiskey, which seemed to have a softening effect. 'It's good liquor,' she said.

'Eight rattlesnake heads to the barrel,' Kitchenbrand replied. 'If your eyeballs don't start bleedin' soon, there's somethin' wrong with you.' She didn't hand the flask back to Kitchenbrand but placed it instead on the ground. She took the canteen and splashed some of the water over her face. 'Here, take this,' Kitchenbrand said, removing his bandanna and handing it to her. She took it and wiped it across her features. The tar smeared but some of it came off. As far as Kitchenbrand could tell, she hadn't been burned.

'Low-down murderin' varmints,' she snarled.

'You're alive,' Kitchenbrand said.

She looked up at him again with her fierce eyes. 'No thanks to those coyotes. And they still got my grandson.'

She began to wipe her face again but soon abandoned the attempt to clean it in favour of trying to pull some of the feathers from her clothes. Kitchenbrand looked up at the sky. The sun was well down.

'Seems to me it's goin' to take a while for you to get anywhere near bein' cleaned up. Why don't I set up camp right here while you get on with the job and then you can tell me just what happened?'

She pulled a few more feathers from her blackened gear without replying. Looking at her, Kitchenbrand was torn between laughter and pity. She was thin as an abandoned cur.

'Figure you could do with some chowder,' he said. 'I got beans, bacon and coffee. Oh, and I got some spare duds. I guess they're maybe a bit large, but I reckon you could do somethin' with 'em.'

She seemed to weigh his words. 'You ain't got tobacco?' she replied. 'I would surely appreciate a quirley.'

Kitchenbrand grinned. 'Could use one myself,' he said. He reached into a pocket and brought out his pouch of Bull Durham. He threw it to the woman. 'Roll yourself a cigarette,' he said, 'while I get my horse.'

'Hope he ain't allergic to feathers,' the woman said.

* * *

By the time Kitchenbrand had got a fire going and cooked the bacon and beans, darkness had fallen. The old woman had made a fair job of cleaning herself up, but she still presented a sorry appearance. When she had eaten and drunk a mug of coffee, she was at least feeling better. She and Kitchenbrand built smokes and leaned back against some rocks.

'Since it seems we're gonna be spendin' the night together,' Kitchenbrand said, 'I guess some introductions might be in order.'

'Don't need to know your name,' the woman said. He told her it anyway. 'Ain't you gonna tell me your name?' he added.

She shrugged her shoulders. 'Guess it don't make any difference either way,' she replied. 'Folks call me old Virginy.'

' "Take me back to old Virginny",' Kitchenbrand quoted. 'Like the song?'

She looked across at him with flashing eyes. 'Which side were you on?' she said unexpectedly.

'If you're referring to the War Between the States, ma'am, I was proud to call myself a Rebel.'

At his words her eyes seemed to soften and the flicker of a smile touched the corner of her mouth. 'You were in it all the way through?'

'Certainly was, ma'am.'

'Maybe you ain't so bad,' she said.

'I recall how after the slaughter at Sharpsburg,' he murmured reflectively, 'General Lee ordered us back across the Potomac and the regimental band switched from playing 'Maryland, My Maryland' to 'Carry me Back To Old Virginny.' If we had only . . . ' He stopped and looked into the old woman's face.

'It was a long time ago now,' she said softly, and for a moment he felt as though their roles had changed, that he was the victim and she was the one offering solace.

'You got a second name?' he asked.

'Garland,' she said.

'That's a nice name. Virginy Garland.

Sounds kinda fresh, like spring.'

His comment evoked a chortle from his companion. 'Ain't nobody said anythin' like that to me before, leastways not in a long time. I figure that's the Forty-rod speakin' we both been drinkin'.'

Kitchenbrand blew out a long stream of smoke and looked up at the stars. Some emotion that he could not define was tugging gently at his throat and chest. Maybe it was something to do with the war. He hadn't thought about it for many a long day. He leaned over and poured fresh coffee into their mugs.

'Maybe you'd better tell me what happened to you,' he said.

'Can't you see?' she replied. 'Ain't it obvious?'

'I can see you've been tarred and feathered some, but that don't tell me why.'

She was silent for a while and then suddenly the fire in her eyes blazed up again.

9

'They wouldn't have been able a few years ago,' she snapped. 'I can still take care of myself, but they caught me cold.'

He waited for a few moments before replying. 'Who were they?' he said. 'And why did they do it?'

'I might be an old worn-out woman,' she replied, 'but I ain't finished with 'em. I'll make 'em pay for what they done.'

Again he allowed time to pass before responding. 'Maybe I can help you there.'

She twisted her head sharply to give him one of her penetrating glances. 'Why do you say that?' she said. 'You don't know nothin' about me. You don't owe me nothin'.'

'Let's just say I don't like to see old ladies tarred and feathered,' he replied. He blew out another ring of smoke. 'Beggin' your pardon for callin' you old, ma'am, but I guess you know what I mean.'

After a moment her face relaxed. 'No

need for apologies,' she replied. 'Like I say, that's what folks call me. Hell, I weren't never any kind of calico queen.' She sat back again, seeming to ponder the situation. 'OK,' she said at length. 'If you really want to know, I'll tell you the story.' She coughed and spat into the fire. 'I reckon you're a stranger to the area?' she said.

Kitchenbrand nodded in agreement. 'Sure am. Passin' through. Leastways, I was.'

'Then you won't have heard of the Yuma gang?'

Kitchenbrand's hand paused on its way to his mouth with the cigarette. 'The Yuma gang?' he repeated.

'Yup. That's what I said.'

His hand resumed its motion and he took a drag. 'Matter of fact I have,' he replied. 'If it's the same bunch, I helped to put a few of 'em behind bars. But that was some time ago.'

'Well, looks like some of 'em musta either busted out or got released and taken to their old ways again.'

'Like I say, if it's the same bunch.' He turned his head sideways. 'Are they the ones responsible for doin' this to you?'

She shook her head. 'No. The ones that did the tarrin' and featherin' did it because they claimed my grandson Ty is one of 'em. They held up a bank in Chaparral Bend. Some people got shot and the manager, Tom Farley, was killed. Folks reckoned Ty was the one responsible. They come for him and took him away.'

'Who took him away? Some of the townsfolk?'

'I reckon so. I thought I recognized one or two of 'em. Don't get up to town too often. The only one I recognized for certain was a man name of Clovis. Landon Clovis. Runs a spread called the Latigo north of Chaparral Bend and owns property in town.'

'Then it weren't no sort of legal posse?'

'Nope. Wouldn't have been. Marshal Purdom is a decent man. He wouldn't hold no truck with somethin' like that.'

'When did this happen?'

'About a week ago.'

'And where is Ty now?'

'They got him in the jailhouse. I know that because I rode in and checked. Figured they might have lynched him. As it is, they're buildin' a gallows high.'

'They took him a week ago,' Kitchenbrand mused. 'So they didn't tar and feather you at the time?'

'Nope. A bunch of 'em came back and did that to me later. I figure they thought I deserved a little punishment too, just for havin' brung him up.'

Kitchenbrand leaned over and absent-mindedly poured himself and Virginy another cup of coffee. He swallowed a mouthful before turning to her. 'And what makes you think he wasn't involved?' he said.

'You mean with the Yuma gang or the bank robbery?'

'Both.'

She hesitated for just a moment. 'I ain't disputin' he was once involved

13

with those Yuma boys. He didn't make much of a secret of it. But that was a whiles ago. I know he come to see the error of his ways. And I know he weren't involved with no robbery because he was home with me at the time it occurred.'

'You sure about that?' Kitchenbrand said.

For a moment, the fire blazed up in her eyes but it quickly died down again. 'Yeah, I'm sure,' she said. 'I know it because the robbery took place on the anniversary of the day he first come to me: June the seventeenth. I'm not likely to forget it. I made us a cake. Besides, I reckon I know my own grandchild. I ain't blind to his faults. I knowed when he was runnin' wild. But I know he's a good boy at heart and that he come to see just where he was goin' wrong.'

'Sounds reasonable to me,' Kitchenbrand replied. He drank some more coffee. 'You say they got him in jail in

Chaparral Bend?' he resumed.

'That's right. They won't let me see him, though.'

'You say they're buildin' a gallows. That ain't encouragin'. Sounds like maybe they already made their minds up about him.'

'That's what I figure. They didn't need no other excuse to come tarrin' and featherin' me.'

'Where exactly do you and your grandson live?' Kitchenbrand said.

'We got our own little place,' she replied. 'Name of the Chicken Track. Don't amount to much, not more than just a shack, but we got us a nice parcel of land. We used to keep some hens. That's why we called it the Chicken Track. We did all right.'

'Is it far from here?' Kithenbrand said.

'Why, no. Those rattlesnakes that run me off didn't carry me too far.'

Kitchenbrand had finished his coffee and threw the dregs on to the fire. 'Seems to me like I need to pay a visit

15

to Chaparral Bend and real quick,' he said. 'We'll start early in the mornin'. I'll take you back to the Chicken Track and then head for town.'

'Why would you do that?'

'I think I already said: I got some objections to an old lady bein' set on.'

'You gonna help my grandson get justice?'

Kitchenbrand shrugged. 'Somethin' like that,' he replied. 'Gonna see for myself what's goin' on.'

'Well, that sounds fine so far as it goes.'

'What are you suggestin'?'

'Nothin'. Only I ain't gonna be left out when you hit Chaparral Bend. I'm comin' with you.'

Kitchenbrand thought over her words for a moment. He looked across at the determined set of her features. 'Yup,' he said. 'I reckon you are.' For the second time Virginy's face relaxed into the semblance of a smile. 'Besides,' Kitchenbrand added, 'I guess I'm gonna need you around to identify those low-down buzzards that tarred and feathered you.'

*   *   *

Kitchenbrand was up before the dawn, awakened by the smell of fatback sizzling in the pan.

'You're awake mighty early,' he said.

'Ain't one to lie abed,' she replied.

When they had eaten they wasted no time in putting out the fire and clearing the camp, leaving as little trace as possible of their occupancy of the site. Kitchenbrand helped hoist the old woman on to the horse's back and then swung up behind her.

'Kinda cosy, ain't it?' she said.

Now that he was close to her, he noticed for the first time that she smelled and he wasn't sure whether it was entirely on account of the tarring and feathering. *She's had a mighty rough time of it*, he reflected. The smell was no worse than a night in the bunkhouse after a hard day on the range and a lot better than riding drag on a herd of longhorns.

They hadn't gone too far when she pointed out a side trail.

'It's a short-cut,' she said. 'The cabin is just on the other side of those low hills.'

He turned the horse and they carried on riding till, coming to the crest of a long rise, she startled him by giving a sudden gasp. 'The cabin,' she exclaimed, pointing ahead. 'It ain't there no more!'

As they rode down the opposite slope he could see the remains of what had been a cabin standing in front of some trees with a trampled vegetable garden in front. His first thought was that the cabin must have been razed but when they got close he could see that it had been physically knocked down. Parts of it still stood upright. Coming to a stop, Kitchenbrand slid from the saddle. He made to help his companion but she had already got down too.

'Goldurn stinkin' coyotes,' she muttered. 'They didn't need to do this.'

Kitchenbrand walked round the piled up layers of debris, pausing at intervals to examine the wreckage. To his practised eye there was plenty of sign indicating that a group of at least half a dozen riders had been that way.

'Looks like they fastened ropes to the frame and then pulled it down using their horses.'

The old woman began searching among the debris but after a few moments stood upright. 'Why should I bother,' she said. 'It didn't, amount to nothin' anyways.'

'It was your home,' Kitchenbrand replied.

'Maybe while Ty was around, but not now they took him away.'

'It can be rebuilt,' Kitchenbrand said.

The old lady's attention seemed to be fixed on something behind him. She was looking towards the trees and Kitchenbrand turned in their direction. Just at that moment there was a sudden agitation among the branches and a crow came wheeling from the foliage, followed by another group of them, diving and cawing. Instinctively Kitchenbrand reached for his gun as something exploded and a shot, came whistling through the air. It went singing by his ear as he squeezed the trigger of his own Colt Frontier revolver. He heard a shout and then a groan and he began to run forward, crouched low, shouting to the old woman as he did so to take cover.

Another shot rang out but it was hopelessly wide. In a further few yards he was among the trees, looking about him for signs of their attacker. He paused to listen and after a minute or two was rewarded by the sound of hoofbeats moving away beyond the trees. He continued running but by the time he emerged again into the open the rapidly fading clatter of galloping hoofs told him the gunman was gone.

He made his way back through the trees, observing as he did so that the ground was spattered at one point with blood. The old woman had not taken his advice but was standing in the open more or less where she had been from the start.

'You got Reba to thank for saving your skin,' she said.

Kitchenbrand was about to expostulate and remind her that it was her property they were on when he became aware that a large crow was sitting on her shoulder.

'Reba?' he repeated dully. 'Who's Reba?'

'This is Reba,' she said, stroking the crow's feathers. 'Guess I'd better introduce you. I rescued her when she were no more than a fledgling and fell out the nest. She's been with me ever since.' She tapped it on the beak. 'Reckon me and Reba are two of a kind.'

Kitchenbrand continued to look at the bird with incomprehension written across his face.

'Reba saved us,' the woman said,

including herself this time. 'She gave the warning just in time.' The crow opened its mouth and gave a loud, raucous caw. 'There you go,' the woman said. 'I reckon she likes you.'

Kitchenbrand glanced about him. He was pretty sure there had only been one gunman, but he couldn't see any point in staying to find out. He put the point to Virginy.

'There won't be anyone else,' she said. 'That ain't Landon Clovis's way.'

'What do you mean,' Kitchenbrand said. 'Do you know who that man was?'

'Nope, but I reckon he'll be one of Landon Clovis's boys. Dry-gulchin' folks is just his style.'

'We got no idea who it was,' Kitchenbrand said. 'Coulda been anybody.'

'We ain't likely to be able to prove it, but I know all the same.'

Kitchenbrand was feeling confused. 'What reason would he have for shootin' at either of us?'

'Landon Clovis don't need no

reason, same way he and the rest of 'em had no reason to tar and feather an old lady. That's just the way they operate.'

'Well, whoever it was,' Kitchenbrand replied, 'he's wounded. There's blood back in the trees.'

'Can't be hurt too bad or he wouldn't have got away,' Virginy said.

Kitchenbrand took a look all around. 'Anything you want to try and save from this mess?' he said.

Virginy shook her head. 'Long as Reba is safe,' she replied. The bird suddenly squawked again and, flapping its wings, rose into the air and flew into the higher branches of a tupelo tree.

'There,' Virginy said. 'She's done her duty and now she's gone back to rest up.'

'Wish we could do the same,' Kitchenbrand replied, 'but we need to get goin'.' Virginy nodded. 'Get back on the horse,' Kitchenbrand said. 'There's nothin' to be done here. The only sensible thing we can do right now is to get to Chaparral Bend.'

They returned to the horse but before mounting it Kitchenbrand turned to the old woman.

'When we get there, the first thing I aim to do is pay the marshal a visit and I don't want you on my coat tails when I do it.'

'Ty is my grandson,' she said. 'I want to see him.'

'Yeah, and so you will. But once we get to town I want you to keep out of the way, at least for the time being. You can book in at the hotel and enjoy its amenities till I tell you otherwise.'

'I'm comin' to Chaparral Bend,' she replied, 'but I ain't stayin' at no hotel. There's an old run-down shack just outside of town will do me fine. Nobody ain't lived there in a long time.'

'Suit yourself,' Kitchenbrand replied. Without waiting any further, he lifted her from the ground and slung her on the horse's back.

'I ain't waitin' for long. If'n you don't get right back and tell me what's happenin' about Ty, I'm comin' right in after you.'

'You know,' Kitchenbrand said, 'I'm beginnin' to think a spot of tarrin' and featherin' might not go amiss myself.'

'Depends on whose doin' it to who,' she replied.

As Kitchenbrand stepped into leather, from the tops of the trees a loud cawing broke on their ears.

They rode steadily, Kitchenbrand's senses alert for any sign of trouble. That shot from the trees worried him. Who could it have been? And was there a connection to everything else that had happened? The more he thought about the woman's story, the more puzzling some of its elements became. There was something peculiarly vicious about the way she had been treated. If her grandson had come under suspicion of robbery and murder, that was one thing. It was understandable that a bunch of townsfolk should have turned up and taken him in. But then why should anyone have come back to tar and feather the old girl and destroy her home? That seemed more like something the Yuma boys might do.

He would need to talk with Virginy again. For some reason he tended to believe her claim in her grandson's innocence but he could be wrong. A lot would depend on how things panned out in Chaparral Bend.

Kitchenbrand hadn't been expecting much, but the shack proved to be even lower than his expectations. It was concealed among a grove of trees and bushes growing alongside a muddy stream and had obviously been abandoned long before. It leaned at an angle and parts of the roof had fallen in. The last remnants of what had been a porch hung lopsidedly and vegetation was rapidly taking over the rest of it.

'Ah, nobody been in it since I was last here,' Virginy said when she had swung down from the horse and pushed wide the already open door.

'You mean you been here before?' Kitchenbrand said.

'Lords a' mercy, I lived here long enough when Ty weren't but a whippersnapper, and I made use of it a few times since. It were in better condition in those days.' She broke off and her face split in a saw-toothed grin. 'There's my old armchair. And there's my old saddle still lyin' in the corner. I'm plumb feelin' at home already.'

Kitchenbrand took another look about at the scene of squalor. 'You sure you wouldn't rather put up at the hotel?' he asked.

'Nope siree. I'll be comfortable as a flea on a hound-dog right here.'

Kitchenbrand was weighing up the situation. 'It ain't far to town,' he said. 'But I figure I'll leave it till the mornin' to ride on in and get some stores. I got stuff in my saddle-bags so we won't need much. I'll get you some clothes too. That shirt of mine ain't exactly befittin'.'

'You don't need to do that,' she replied. 'Might get folks talkin', you comin' away with female garments. But

27

I thought we agreed not to waste any time.'

'One night ain't gonna make a difference.' He moved towards the open door. 'Sure you'll be OK?' he said.

'I been lookin' out for myself for more than sixty years,' she replied. 'Don't need no greener to start worryin' about me.'

Kitchenbrand grinned. 'See you later then,' he said.

He wasn't planning to spend any time in the shack. It might suit the old lady, but he intended setting up camp right beside the stream. Then in the morning the first thing he would do would be to pay that visit to the marshal.

2

There was something about Kitchen-brand that made people stop what they were doing and look. It would be hard to say just what it was. There was nothing unusual or prepossessing about his appearance, nothing striking about the way he dressed. Maybe it was an aura of calm that surrounded him.

He rode the roan gelding and when he reached the place where the gallows was being built, he stopped and looked up at it for a good few minutes. The town carpenter was putting the finishing touches to it, sitting high on the crossbeam hammering in nails. He halted in mid-swing and looked down at the stranger. The two exchanged glances before Kitchenbrand carried on riding as far as the marshal's office, where he swung down and tied the horse to the hitchrack. His glance swept up and down the street and then, with a rap on the door, he stepped inside.

The marshal was reclining with his feet on his desk but he put them on the floor and sat up when Kitchenbrand entered. He put his hands on the desk in front of him as if to rise.

'Seems like there's gonna be a hangin',' Kitchenbrand said.

The marshal was nonplussed. He didn't know how to take the intrusion. He observed that the stranger wore his gun butt foremost on his left hip.

'What's that to you?' he said.

Kitchenbrand's eyes glanced up to a door at the back of the room which gave entry to the cells and then rested on the marshal. 'You got a boy in there called Ty Garland,' he said. The marshal didn't say anything either to confirm or deny the statement. 'Some say he robbed the bank and shot somebody. He didn't do it,' Kitchenbrand concluded.

The marshal grunted. 'Now that's mighty interestin',' he replied. 'But a lot of folk think different.'

'Then they got it wrong,' Kitchenbrand said.

Despite his abrupt manner, the marshal was beginning to feel more comfortable. 'I don't think I caught your name,' he said.

'You don't need to know it.'

'Just the same, if you and I are goin' to get any further with this, I'd appreciate havin' it.'

'Name's Kitchenbrand, Hollis Kitchenbrand.'

'Hollis Kitchenbrand,' the marshal repeated. It seemed to him that he had heard the name before but he couldn't think where. 'OK, Mr Kitchenbrand. Just to complete the introductions, I'm Marshal Purdom.'

'I'd like to see the boy,' Kitchenbrand said.

This time the marshal did get to his feet. 'I'm sure you would,' he said, 'but it wouldn't be sensible for me to let you do that until I know just what this is all about.'

Kitchenbrand gave the marshal a

searching look, then nodded. His attitude seemed to soften. 'I guess that's fair,' he said.

For the first time the marshal noticed his dusty clothes. 'Been ridin'?' he said. Without waiting for an answer, he continued. 'How about you and me step over to the saloon. I reckon you could maybe do with a drink.'

The shadow of a smile passed over Kitchenbrand's features. 'Coffee would be better,' he said.

They were about to step outside when the marshal stopped and turned to Kitchenbrand. 'Oh, one thing before we leave,' he said.

'Yeah, what's that?' Kitchenbrand replied.

'I'd better take your guns. There's a new rule in Chaparral Bend. No guns in public places. Introduced it myself.'

Kitchenbrand seemed to hesitate a moment before undoing the buckle of his gunbelt. He handed it to the marshal, who hung it on a stand in a corner of the room.

'OK,' Purdom said, 'after you, Mr Kitchenbrand.'

They went out and the marshal locked the door behind them. The sounds of hammering reached their ears as they strode across the street to an establishment outside of which a rather grandiose sign read *Fashion Restaurant and Coffee Shop*. Inside, the place at least seemed to make some effort at respectability. There were tables with blue-checked cloths and flowers in vases. A woman in a blue gingham dress greeted the marshal.

'Hello, Mr Purdom.' She glanced at Kitchenbrand.

'Hello, Bella,' the marshal replied. 'Seems kinda quiet today.'

'It's been like that recently. Looks like folks is keepin' away from town.'

There was an unspoken meaning to her words but Kitchenbrand guessed it had something to do with the gallows. They took a seat near a window, the marshal taking care that he had a clear view of the street outside.

'If you're hungry, I can recommend Bella's steak pie,' he said.

'Kinda early for me,' Kitchenbrand replied. 'Coffee would be fine.'

The marshal ordered coffee for them both. There was silence till it arrived and then it was Kitchenbrand who spoke. He didn't bother with preliminaries but went straight to the point.

'Ty Garland is innocent. He got in with a bad crowd. It was the Yuma gang that did the robbery and the shootin'.'

'There are witnesses. They will identify Garland.'

'More likely they are angry people who can be persuaded to make false statements.'

'You got reasons for sayin' that?'

'Nope. But I think there's more to it. You ever hear of an *hombre* by the name of Angel Addison?' The marshal looked blank. He wasn't giving anything away. 'He's leader of the Yuma gang. I've got a feelin' he's the one who should be in that jailhouse. I know the way Addison and the Yuma gang operate. I was responsible for puttin' some of 'em in the Yuma penitentiary in the first place.'

The marshal looked up at the stranger. 'I knew I'd heard the name before,' he said. 'You're Crossdraw Kitchenbrand, the man who cleaned out Eagleton.'

Kitchenbrand wiped his mouth with a napkin. 'Some damn fool people called me that. Figure it's just a lot of tomfoolery myself.' He finished his coffee and sat back. The marshal produced a pouch of tobacco and they built smokes.

'What's your relation to Ty Garland?' Purdom asked.

Kitchenbrand inhaled deeply and blew out smoke from his nostrils. 'Let's just say I got an interest in justice bein' served.'

The marshal looked steadily at Kitchenbrand as he drank the last dregs of his coffee.

'You still haven't said what makes

you think Ty Garland don't deserve to hang.'

'I heard tell he was somewhere else on the night of the robbery.'

'Can anyone vouch for that?'

'Yes. Someone I happen to believe.'

The marshal's face relaxed and almost broke into a smile. 'Now you ain't tellin' me you've been talkin' to Virginy Garland?'

'She ain't denyin' Ty got tangled up with those Yuma boys. But the first she knew any thin' about the robbery was when the posse turned up at her door.'

Just as the marshal was about to say something further there were sounds of a disturbance outside. He looked out of the window. A lot of people had suddenly appeared and were swarming down the street in the direction of his office.

'Somethin's happenin',' he said. He leaped to his feet and made for the door. Kitchenbrand took a last draw on his cigarette, stubbed it out in an ashtray, and walked over to the counter.

'That was real good coffee,' he said. 'How much do I owe you?'

When he had paid he strode to the door and out into the sunlight. A large group of people had congregated outside the marshal's office and he appeared to be arguing with those at the front. Kitchenbrand stepped off the boardwalk. People were shouting and as he got closer he could make out what they were saying.

'Hand him over, Marshal!'

'Hangin's too good for that low-down son of a skunk.'

He heard the marshal's reply as he tried to make himself heard over the gathering tumult. 'Let the law take its course. Get back to your business.'

Towards the back of the crowd Kitchenbrand observed a number of mean looking individuals who seemed to be urging the crowd on.

'Get out of our way, Marshal,' another voice shouted. 'Don't waste your time tryin' to defend the varmint.'

'We mean to have him. What can one

man do? Be sensible and get out of our way.'

Kitchenbrand took a little detour around the crowd and then stepped up to the boardwalk alongside the marshal. 'He ain't one man now,' he said.

'Don't pay him no mind,' the voice called. 'He ain't even got a gun.'

Kitchenbrand's arm was behind his back. Now he swung it forward. In his hand was the Sharps rifle he had just taken from its scabbard in front of his saddle.

'Like the marshal said, go on back to where you came from and let the law take its course.'

The crowd still remained but a change could be detected. People weren't quite so sure as they had been and one or two began slowly to drift away.

'Go on!' the marshal shouted. 'This ain't no way to go about things.'

A few more people began to shift and shuffle. Suddenly there was a crackle from the back of the mob and a bullet flew past Kitchenbrand's ear, smashing the window of a shop behind him. People began to shout and scream as the mob started to scatter. The marshal's revolver was in his hand as his eyes searched for the person who had fired the shot.

Another shot rang out from somewhere over their heads. Instantly Kitchenbrand's rifle roared and from the roof of a building opposite a man came crashing headlong to the ground. The townsfolk were panicking now and running in all directions. The men Kitchenbrand had spotted at the back of the crowd seemed to have disappeared like smoke. He had no doubt in his mind that it was one of them who had fired the first shot but he had managed to make good his escape.

'Get inside,' Kitchenbrand rapped, 'in case there's any more of 'em.'

They slammed inside the office and took their places by the window, peering out at the street. The excitement seemed to have died down. A few people still remained but most of them had fled. Kitchenbrand looked up at the roof line but he could see no further sign of activity. After waiting for another five minutes the marshal stepped to the door and, standing to one side, opened it. Nothing happened.

'Cover me,' he said.

Kitchenbrand moved swiftly across to the doorway and the marshal ducked outside. There was no response. After a few moments he came back inside. 'Looks like that's it,' he said.

'Yeah. For now.'

The marshal reached into his desk and brought out a bottle of bourbon which he proceeded to pour into two glasses.

'I don't get it,' he said. 'I don't remember the townsfolk ever actin' that way.'

'It happens,' Kitchenbrand replied. 'I've seen the same thing before. Especially if there are a few outsiders to stir things up.'

'What? Troublemakers?'

'I guess you didn't notice 'em,' Kitchenbrand replied. 'There were some ornery lookin' varmints among that crowd. I figure they could be worse than troublemakers. I figure they could be members of the Yuma gang.'

The marshal took a long swig of the whiskey. 'I figure that kind of proves somethin',' he said.

'Yeah? What does it prove?'

'Well, at least it goes to show that Garland is definitely tied in with 'em.'

'Yeah, but what were they after? Lynchin' him?'

The marshal swallowed another mouthful of the whiskey. 'Why would they do that? Garland's due to hang anyway.'

Kitchenbrand shrugged. 'I don't know. Besides, doesn't that depend on the judge? You got Garland behind bars. Why don't you ask him?'

The marshal looked up at Kitchenbrand. 'Say, you only once mentioned seein' the boy since you got here. You want to talk to him now?'

41

'Later,' Kitchenbrand said. He glanced at his gunbelt hanging on the stand. 'You don't mind if I have that back?' he added.

'It's against my policy,' the marshal said with a grin. 'But I guess there are exceptional circumstances.'

Kitchenbrand fastened the gunbelt round his waist and had begun to move towards the door when he stopped.

'If I'm right,' he said, 'and those varmints I saw in the crowd are some of the Yuma gang, you can bet there'll be more of 'em around, and you can also bet they'll make another attempt at gettin' Garland out of here.'

The marshal nodded. 'Yeah, I figure you could be right.'

'Maybe it would be an idea for me to stick around a while,' Kitchenbrand said.

'You could try the Matagorda hotel,' the marshal replied.

Kitchenbrand nodded. He saw no reason to mention Virginy's shack. 'See you later,' he said.

Ty Garland had heard the commotion going on outside the marshal's office and when shooting began, he knew it was something fairly serious. It was useless to try and see through the small barred opening high in the wall. There was no way he could haul himself up to it so he had to content himself with listening. It was hard to make anything out but he could hear voices raised in anger and suddenly he realized that it was a lynch mob. Only the marshal stood between himself and an agonizing death. He began to pace up and down in agitation but presently the noise died down and then it was quiet once more. Quiet, that was, except for the incessant sound of hammering which soon began again in the square outside. He sat down on the bare iron frame which served as a bed and buried his head in his hands. The odds had been stacked against him from the start.

After the last robbery the townsfolk

had been angry and ready to blame any scapegoat. It wasn't so much for himself as for his grandmother that he felt pain and regret. She had done her best to bring him up alone after his father had died. She had tried to make him see the error of his ways but he had ignored her pleas. He realized now how foolish he had been ever to get involved with the Yuma gang. This was what it led to: four bare walls and a gallows tree.

After leaving the marshal Kitchenbrand rode his horse to the livery stable, then visited the barbershop where he had a bath and shave. He wandered about the town for a while and had almost decided to return to the shack where he had left Virginy when he changed his mind and made his way back to the marshal's office instead. Purdom was still there.

'There was somethin' I forgot to ask,' Kitchenbrand said.

'Yeah? What was that?'

'Is there a day fixed for the trial?'

'Not yet,' the marshal said. 'How did you get involved in this anyway? Was I right about Virginy Garland?'

'I ain't denyin' it. And by the way, it seems some of your townsmen weren't content to take her grandson. A bunch of 'em turned up later and tarred and feathered her. What's more, they tore down her house as well.'

There was no mistaking the marshal's expression of shock and disbelief, but Kitchenbrand didn't want to pursue the matter. There was something of more immediate importance on his mind. Without pause, he continued: 'I got a proposition to make.'

'I'm listenin',' Purdom replied after a moment.

'I may be entirely wrong about this, but I don't think so. That crowd earlier was stoked up by some of the Yuma gang.'

'So you say,' the marshal replied.

'It didn't work,' Kitchenbrand continued, ignoring the marshal's comment,

45

'but they ain't gonna leave it at that. Which means they're gonna try somethin' else. My money's on 'em goin' for tonight, while they're in town.'

The marshal ran his hand over his chin, weighing up Kitchenbrand's words. 'I been thinkin' too,' he said, 'and I reckon you got a point.'

'Good. That leaves two options. Either we hunker down and prepare to defend this place against whatever the Yuma boys are plannin' to throw at it. Or . . . '

'Or what?' Purdom interposed.

'We remove Garland from here to somewhere safe that the Yuma gang ain't gonna know nothin' about.'

The marshal's brow was puckered in concentration as he pondered Kitchenbrand's words. 'What you say makes sense, but how do I know it ain't some elaborate plot to spring him yourself?'

'You don't. You're gonna just have to take it on trust.'

'He ain't gonna hang till he's been convicted.'

'Tell that to the next necktie party.'

Purdom considered his words. 'You want me to give you time?' he said.

'When I came here I didn't have a clear idea about just what I intended to do, but I certainly wasn't meanin' to try and spring Garland myself. If I'd planned on doin' that, I wouldn't have come straight to see you.'

'What did you expect to achieve?'

'I don't know. I just kinda figured someone'd see sense.' Kitchenbrand paused and looked at Purdom. 'It ain't for me to say,' he continued, 'but I'm thinkin' maybe I found that person.'

Purdom got to his feet and walked to the window where he spent a few moments looking out on the street. When he turned back there was determination written across his features.

'OK,' he said. 'There are some things about all this I don't like. Matter of fact, I got my deputy, Bert Hardy, doin' some checkin'. Talkin' to you has made me realize it even more. I don't know just exactly what the right and wrongs of it all are, but I go along with you this far. Let's get Garland out of here.'

Without waiting for a reply, he took a set of keys from the drawer of his desk and unlocked the interconnecting door. There was a short corridor between his office and the cells. With Kitchenbrand just behind him, he walked through.

There were two cells, only one of which was occupied. When he heard the door opening, Garland got to his feet and came to the front of his cell with fists clenched, fearing for a moment that it might be the lynch mob come to get him. When he perceived it was the marshal his features relaxed but when he saw another man behind he instinctively took up a defensive stance again.

'It's OK,' Purdom said. 'This man is called Kitchenbrand. You might say he's one of my deputies.'

'What was all that noise earlier?' Garland asked.

'Some folks tryin' to take the law into

their own hands. That's why we're here. We're movin' you somewhere safe just in case anyone feels like tryin' it again.'

Garland looked suspiciously at Kitchenbrand. It was dark inside the cells compared to the marshal's office and Purdom could not see the expression on Kitchenbrand's face.

'We're doin' this for your own good,' Purdom said. 'I trust you to cooperate.'

'I told you, I had nothin' to do with that robbery. I ain't gonna cause no trouble.'

'Then just do whatever I tell you,' the marshal said, 'but remember. No funny business.' He unlocked the door and the three of them returned to the front office.

'Where are we goin'?' Garland said.

Kitchenbrand had been wondering the same thing.

'For the time bein', we're goin' to my place,' Purdom replied. He went to the window and glanced out. The street was relatively quiet. He came back and reached into a drawer.

'Here, put. this on,' he said to Garland, producing an old battered Stetson. When Garland pulled it down low, his face was pretty well concealed. The marshal stepped to the door and opened it carefully. 'All clear,' he said.

They slipped through the doorway into the street. The marshal quickly locked the door. 'OK, follow me.'

He turned and began to walk down the street in the opposite direction to that in which he had accompanied Kitchenbrand to the restaurant. They were moving away from the centre of town and after a few minutes the marshal led them down an alley and through some deserted streets. They took another turn and kept walking till the marshal brought them to a halt.

'This is my place,' he said.

They were standing by a white picket fence. Behind it stood a single storey house with a veranda running round three sides. Kitchenbrand could hear the faint sound of running water somewhere beyond it. Purdom opened a gate and they went up a path leading to the front porch. He opened the door and they slipped inside.

'Nothin' to it,' he said.

He closed some curtains and lit a lamp. The room was suffused in a warm roseate glow. Kitchenbrand looked about him. Although it was sparsely furnished, the room looked comfortable.

'Bella occasionally does some cleaning,' Purdom said. 'You know, the lady you met at the restaurant. I do my own cookin'.'

'It's a nice set-up,' Kitchenbrand remarked.

Garland had remained silent, but now, taking off the Stetson, he spoke briefly. 'Thanks for this, Marshal,' he said. 'And you, Mr Kitchenbrand. I sure appreciate it.'

'Just remember what I said,' Purdom responded. 'Don't try anything clever.'

'Whatever you say,' Garland replied.

'This arrangement is temporary,' Purdom said. 'There's a spare room through the back. I'll show you in a minute.'

Kitchenbrand took this as his cue. 'Reckon I'll be goin',' he said.

The marshal looked surprised. 'I thought you intended stayin'. In view of what we were talkin' about and all.' Purdom had the feeling that now they had reached his house in safety, Kitchenbrand was feeling awkward.

'There won't be any trouble tonight,' Kitchenbrand said. 'Nobody knows Ty Garland is here.' He turned to the youngster. 'You keep your head down. Don't take any chances of someone spottin' you.'

The marshal thought his voice sounded slightly strained. 'Come over first thing in the mornin',' he said. 'We'll need to decide what to do next.'

'Sure. See you both tomorrow.'

Kitchenbrand turned and walked out through the door. When he was back in the street he paused once to look back before directing his steps towards the livery stable.

* * *

It was late in the afternoon when he got back to the shack. He was leading an extra horse, which he had acquired from the livery stable for Virginy. For a moment he caught a glimpse of her face at the window, then she appeared on the rickety porch. She was looking quite a lot different from the way she had been and was wearing a grey calico dress that she must have found in the shack. She had cleaned off the last of the tar and her lank hair was tied behind in a bun.

'Well, what's the news?' she said. 'You seen my grandson?'

Kitchenbrand swung down from the saddle. 'Let me attend to the horses,' he replied, 'and then I'll tell you exactly what's happened.'

When he got back inside the shack he could smell food cooking and realized for the first time that he had had nothing to eat or drink since having coffee earlier that morning with Marshal Purdom.

He suddenly felt hungry.

'Sit down,' Virginy said. 'I figure you could put away some grub.'

She had made a stew, to be accompanied by black coffee and sourdough biscuits. She certainly knew how to cook. As they ate Kitchenbrand told her what had occurred in town. As he talked she broke in every now and then with muted expletives. When he had finished her face was flushed.

'They're tryin' to lynch him?' she said. 'Hell, what are we waitin' for? Let's go right in and get him.'

'That ain't the way to handle things,' Kitchenbrand said. 'Your grandson's safe with the marshal for tonight. I've arranged to go back in the mornin' and talk over the situation with Purdom. You're right about him. He's a decent man. He ain't happy with things himself. The best way to handle this is to cooperate with him.'

'Then I'm comin' with you,' she said.

'I ain't got no problem with that.'

He produced his tobacco pouch.

They each rolled a cigarette.

'You know,' he said, 'there's one thing been puzzlin' me. If I'm right about some of the Yuma gang bein' behind that lynch mob, I can't see what they would stand to gain by it. Why would they want to stir up the crowd? Why would they want a lynchin'?'

'Ain't that obvious? They knew Ty weren't guilty. They musta wanted him out of the way in case he persuaded the marshal to see things that way.'

'You could be right, but I figure there's more to it. I reckon they were hopin' to spring him in the confusion. I reckon it was a rescue attempt.'

'What are you implyin'? That I'm lyin' and that Ty is one of the gang?'

'I didn't say that.' He paused for a few seconds. 'Although it would fit.'

Virginy got to her feet. 'Go on, git,' she shouted. 'You're no different from all the rest of those low-down ornery rattlesnakes. I never shoulda trusted you.'

'Simmer down,' Kitchenbrand said.

'All I said was that it would fit one interpretation of the situation. I didn't say I believed it.'

The old lady hesitated, struggling with her feelings before sitting down again. 'You'd better not be stringin' me along,' she muttered.

Kitchenbrand got to his feet and went over to his saddle-bags. He produced the bottle of whiskey. 'Here,' he said, 'I figure we could both do with something a little stronger.'

He poured each of them a stiff shot. The old woman threw her head back and swallowed half the glass. She shivered. 'Yeah, that's better,' she said.

He topped her glass up again before returning to the conversation. 'OK,' he said. 'I believe you when you tell me that Ty is innocent. If I'm right, that means those Yuma boys were eggin' on the crowd so they could intervene and set him free. They must have a reason for wantin' to do that.'

The old woman did not say anything this time and Kitchenbrand's thoughts ran on. 'There's somethin' else I been thinkin',' he said. 'I assumed that the varmints who came back and tarred and feathered you were the same ones who came and took your grandson. Now I'm pretty sure they weren't. I'm just about certain they must have been some of the Yuma boys too.'

'Could be,' Virginy said after thinking for a moment. 'I sure didn't recognize any of 'em.'

'And you did recognize some of the first ones?'

'Yeah. Like I said, that schemin' son of a gun Landon Clovis in particular.'

'Why do you say that?'

'Because I never trusted him. He tried to get hold of the Chicken Track once before but I wasn't havin' any of it.'

'He offered you money?'

'Yes, and probably more than the property's worth. But I wasn't gonna sell out my home to no one.'

'Maybe there's some sort of tie-in between this *hombre* Clovis and the Yuma gang?'

'I never heard of Clovis gettin' involved with anythin' outside the law,' Virginy said. 'He's too sly, too clever. It ain't the way he operates.'

'Maybe he's sly enough to convince everybody that's the case,' Kitchenbrand said. 'Maybe a little chat with Marshal Purdom might throw some light on his operations.'

'You can talk to Purdom, but he won't tell you anythin' different.'

'That bushwhacker I shot,' Kitchenbrand mused. 'I figure the rest of the bunch quitted the Chicken Track not long before we turned up. He must have been hangin' around for some reason and saw us comin'. Thought he'd have a little fun takin' a pot shot at me.'

'Or maybe me,' Virginy said. 'Lucky for us both that Reba was there to keep an eye on things.'

Kitchenbrand didn't respond. Who knew, maybe the old girl was right? Probably the crows had been disturbed by his movement, or maybe the shine of his gun.

'I'm gettin' kinda tired tryin' to work this all out,' Kitchenbrand said. 'Maybe things will become a bit clearer after we've seen the marshal tomorrow. That grandson of yourn is sure gonna get a surprise when he sees you walk in.'

Virginy's eyes were shining in the light of a lamp. Kitchenbrand thought he saw the glimmer of a tear.

'He's only a boy,' she said. 'Landogoshen, he ain't had much of a chance with only me to keep an eye out for him.'

Kitchenbrand smiled. 'I figure he coulda done a lot worse,' he said.

3

Kitchenbrand woke early the next morning and made his way to the shack. Virginy was already up and about and had bacon and beans sizzling in the pan.

'Couldn't sleep,' she said. 'I kept thinkin' about Ty. I just hope you're right about workin' with the marshal.'

He ate quickly and then fed and saddled the horses. Virginy was anxious to be gone but Kitchenbrand pointed out that the marshal was not likely to be expecting him at so early an hour.

Eventually they rode out, following the trail Kitchenbrand had ridden. It was still earlier than Kitchenbrand would have preferred, but even as they approached the marshal's house he realized that something was wrong. The front door was open and he could see what looked like blood on the front porch.

'Wait here,' he snapped, 'while I find out what's goin' on.'

He leaped from the saddle and ran forward, drawing his six-gun as he did so. Virginy ignored his instruction and followed behind. He flung himself through the doorway. There was more blood on the carpet and evidence of a struggle having taken place in the main room; chairs were scattered, a settee had been upended and there was glass on the floor. There was no sign of either the marshal or his prisoner.

'Purdom!' Kitchenbrand shouted.

The door leading to the room where Garland was to have spent the night was open and Kitchenbrand ran inside. The first thing he noticed was that the window looking out on the garden had been smashed. Then he saw Purdom lying face down on the floor in a pool of blood. He sprang to his side and carefully turned him over.

Purdom was still breathing but he

was in a bad way. He had been shot in the chest and there was a bad gash on the back of his head. There was no sign of Ty Garland. It was obvious that Purdom needed a doctor and quick. Laying the marshal's head down, he was about to make for the front door when he became aware of Virginy behind him.

'What's happened to Ty?' she shouted.

'I don't know. The marshal's been hurt. Stay here while I run and get a doctor.'

'I'll go,' Virginy said. 'You don't know the town. I know where to find Doc Groves.'

She turned and set off at a surprisingly brisk pace. Kitchenbrand got to his feet and took a quick look at the rest of the house. He returned to the room where the marshal lay and it seemed no time at all till he heard the rush of footsteps and Virginy ran in with a grey-haired wiry man right behind her.

'I'm Doc Groves,' he said.

He kneeled down beside the prostrate form of the marshal. After checking him over, he glanced up at Kitchenbrand.

'I think we got to him in the nick of time,' he said. He turned to Virginy. 'Get some towels and some hot water. I'm gonna need your help while I operate.'

Kitchenbrand left the doctor and Virginy to deal with the marshal and took a look outside. He found sign of four horses. He figured that three riders must have been involved in freeing Garland. The other horse must have been for Garland's use. What did that mean in terms of Garland's innocence? It seemed there was only one conclusion to be drawn, but somehow he still found a strange reluctance to concede the youngster's guilt. After a time the doctor and Virginy appeared.

'It was lucky you found him when you did,' the doctor said. 'The actual damage isn't as bad as I thought, but if he had been left much longer he would have died of shock and loss of blood. I've removed the bullet and cleaned the wound. The best thing for him now is rest.'

'What about the head injury?' Kitchenbrand said.

'I'd say someone hit him with the butt of a pistol. It's a nasty gash but not much more.'

'Did he come round?'

'Only briefly. He was in no condition to take anything in.' The doctor looked at Kitchenbrand with suspicion. 'The marshal has obviously been set upon in his own home. Do you know anything about it?'

'Nope. I found him this way.' Kitchenbrand didn't go into any further explanations and the doctor did not press him.

'I'll arrange for Bella Mayes to come over and keep an eye on him.' If the doctor was baffled by Virginy's presence, he did not show it.

While he was talking to the doctor, Kitchenbrand was thinking rapidly. It could only be a short time before the whole town knew what had happened. They would soon realize that Garland was gone from the jailhouse. Things could get awkward. He had done what he could for Purdom and there remained only one thing further that he could do, and that was to find Garland. He owed it to the marshal to track him down and bring him in. The situation had changed dramatically. Whatever the outcome might have been if Purdom had not been attacked was beside the point, now. Innocent or guilty, Garland needed to be found.

He tried not to dwell on the question of whether Garland had betrayed him. He felt a strong sense of guilt. It had been his idea to free the youngster. He didn't just owe it to Purdom, he owed it to himself to deal with Garland.

The big question was whether Garland had carried out the assault himself or whether he had been assisted. From what Kitchenbrand had been able to deduce, it looked as though others had been involved. The fact that some of the Yuma boys had been in town suggested it was them. But how had they known that Garland had been transferred to the marshal's house? Come to that, why would the Yuma gang be interested in trying to free Garland in the first place?

It was the same question that he had asked himself already. Wouldn't they be more likely to have just let him hang? Whatever the answers might be to those questions, finding the Yuma gang was the obvious starting point.

Once he had received the doc's assurances, Kitchenbrand made the decision that there was no point in wasting time. When the doctor had left to fetch Bella Mayes, he outlined his proposal to Virginy.

'I don't care how it looks,' she said, 'my grandson is innocent. He didn't have nothin' to do with this.'

'We ain't got time to argue the point,' Kitchenbrand replied. 'Pretty soon there's gonna be a heap of folk here and they'll all be pointin' the finger. If we don't leave right now, we might find it hard to get another chance. And you ain't exactly popular around town to start with.'

Virginy nodded. 'Let's get movin',' she said.

Well before rumours began to spread, Kitchenbrand and Virginy had left Chaparral Bend behind them.

They kept riding till they had put some distance between themselves and the town. Then they continued to drift southwards, allowing their horses to go at their own pace. After continuing that way for a while, Virginy rode her horse up close to Kitchenbrand's.

'You got any idea where we're goin'?' she said.

'Yeah,' Kitchenbrand replied. 'I might be wrong, but I got a hunch.'

From his experiences with the Yuma gang of old, Kitchenbrand knew the sort of place they would be likely to seek as a base of operations and his instinct told him where it could be. He had heard talk about an almost

67

inaccessible valley to the south-west which was reputed to be connected by obscure trails to other renegade roosts. It was a fair bet that the Yuma gang would be somewhere in the vicinity.

'Do you reckon you can find it?' Virginy asked.

'I reckon so. But I ain't sure what we'll do once we get there.'

'Time enough to worry about that,' Virginy replied. 'Consarnit, we got troubles enough to occupy us before we ever get there.'

As they rode, Kitchenbrand kept his eyes open for sign that might have been made by a sizeable group of riders. It didn't take him long to discover it. It was still quite fresh and, as he had surmised, the tracks led in the general direction of Buzzard Valley. There were plenty of other indications that a number of riders had passed that way: cigarette butts, a discarded canteen.

A little further on they came to a place where the riders had obviously made camp. They had probably ridden out in the small hours and stopped around mid-morning. The ashes still held vestiges of heat. It was clear that at least half a dozen people had been there.

'Guess we're on the right track,' he said.

After they had examined the traces of the camp, they mounted up and continued to ride till the sun was low in the sky, when they found a suitable spot to rest up.

One thing Kitchenbrand was not too concerned about was the matter of provisions. Long experience of riding the trails had taught him the wisdom of being prepared and he had supplies in his saddlebags. Even so, he reflected, it would have been useful if they could have brought a few more things from the shack.

He built a fire and threw some bacon into the pan. When they had eaten they sat back with a tin mug of coffee and a cigarette in their hands. The night was a black veil diamonded with stars. A soft wind blew up from the prairie and rustled through the leaves of the trees. Tethered just out of reach of the firelight, the horses snorted and then were quiet. An owl hooted.

'You know,' Virginy said, 'if it weren't for worryin' about what's become of Ty, I could be quite content.'

'Yeah. I know what you mean. Kinda peaceful, ain't it?'

'You feel more comfortable out in the open than with a roof over your head, don't you?'

'You referrin' to my campin' out the last couple of nights rather than spendin' time in the shack?'

'Yes, but not just that.'

Kithchenbrand suddenly broke into a laugh. 'Never quite figured it this way,' he said.

★　★　★

A little earlier that same evening and a hundred miles away, another man was contemplating his situation. Angel Addison was so named because of his

70

youthful and innocent-looking features, but it would be hard to think of a more inappropriate sobriquet. The man was a killer and it was not by accident that he had fought his way to becoming leader of the notorious Yuma gang.

The gang was named after the fact that Angel and a good few of the others had spent time in the dreaded Yuma penitentiary, the most hated penal institution in the south-west. Its high adobe walls, guard towers and Gatling gun had not been enough to prevent Angel escaping. He had no intention of going back.

As he sat on the veranda of the hut that he called his headquarters he was quietly complimenting himself on the fact that it was highly unlikely the law would ever be able to find him in his mountain valley fastness, where a shanty town of shacks and adobe huts had grown to accommodate him and his owlhoot crew. The settlement was really quite a sight; there were even a couple of saloons and stores and he had dignified it with a name: Addisonville.

The sun was sinking behind the mountains and although there weren't many people about, sounds of revelry floated up from the street below as some of the owlhoots blew off steam. He turned to the woman sitting beside him.

'Let's you and me have some fun,' he said.

She looked down at the scene below. 'I am feeling tired,' she replied. 'Do we have to go down and join those others?'

'Nope, we sure don't.'

She smiled and, getting to her feet, came and sat on his knee. She put her head close to his.

'You mean that? Just you and your Delta? None of the other girls?'

'Just you and me,' he replied. 'I got somethin' special in mind and this time it's all for you.'

She drew her head back and gave him a quizzical look. Just at that moment a shot rang out and involuntarily she flinched.

'It's just one of the boys havin' some fun,' he said. His hand had just moved between her legs when there came a second shot. He grinned. 'That ain't any of the boys down there in town,' he said. 'That's Pike on guard atop the pass, lettin' off a warnin' shot. Looks like we got visitors.' He pushed her aside and rose to his feet. 'Go on in,' he said, 'I won't be long.'

The girl straightened her dress and made her way inside the cabin. Addison turned and leaned on the balustrade. Presently a rider came into sight. He rode into the yard, dismounted and approached Addison.

'We got him, boss!' he shouted.

'Good work, Yager!'

'The boys are bringin' him in. I rode on ahead to tell you the news.'

'What sort of state is he in?'

'Don't worry. He's still in one piece.'

When the man had gone, Addison remained on the veranda a little longer. Now that Garland had been brought in, things were really looking up. He thought about Garland for a few more moments, then he turned and made his way into the cabin. Garland could wait. Delta was waiting for him and he had a few things in mind for her that might surprise even Yager and the boys if they knew.

★　★　★

Late the following day Kitchenbrand and Virginy reached the foothills of the Buzzard range. It had taken them longer than expected because the country was new to both of them and the tracks Kitchenbrand had been following were harder to discern on the rocky ground. At this point he couldn't be sure that he was still on the right track as the trail seemed to lead straight towards a seemingly impassable wall of rock. When they reached it they found a narrow cleft that led into a canyon. The walls were high at first but soon dropped so that the canyon became a small valley. They rode through it till

74

they reached a point where a narrow side trail led them up and then alongside the hill.

Darkness was descending when they drew to a halt and dismounted. They hobbled the horses and then proceeded on foot. Kitchenbrand was pretty sure that Addison would have set guards to keep watch on the usual way through to the valley, assuming he wasn't altogether wrong. Even those precautions were probably unnecessary as the trail would be barely known to anyone but the owlhoots who made use of it.

Kitchenbrand climbed to the crest of a rise from where he could look down on a wide expanse of terrain. As he did so he felt his chest tighten. He wasn't wrong after all. Below him and a little distance away stood a collection of rude buildings which he guessed constituted the robbers' roost he was looking for. Most of them were congregated together along a line which formed a rough and ready main street but there were others scattered about the lower slopes of the surrounding hills. He watched closely for some time but there was no sign of movement.

As night descended Kitchenbrand expected to see some lights appear but the place gave every indication of being deserted. He watched for a little while longer and then, when he had satisfied himself as to its layout, he returned to where he had left the horses with Virginy. In a few words, he outlined what he had seen.

'Seems to me we got two choices,' he said. 'Either we try to sneak into the roost or we just ride in under cover of dark.'

'Goldurn it, I ain't never been one for sneakin' about.'

'OK, but we still keep to the back trail and try to avoid any guards.'

He didn't like to admit to a feeling of disappointment. Had he got things wrong after all? There seemed to be little evidence of any activity. All the same, it would be wise to exercise caution. He hoisted himself into the saddle and together they rode on. Night had fallen but the starlight was enough for their horses to pick their way. They crested the hill and then began to move slowly down towards the settlement. A breeze blew down from the mountains and the horses, scenting something, tossed their heads and sidestepped. Kitchenbrand signalled for them to stop.

They sat for a while, watching and listening. They could see and hear nothing, but even if the place was occupied, they probably wouldn't have picked up any sounds because the wind was blowing the wrong way. When he was satisfied that it was safe to continue, Kitchenbrand motioned with his hand for them to proceed.

They continued to angle their way down the hillside. When they reached level ground they were about a hundred yards from the nearest cabin. The track was well marked, which showed that use had been made of it very recently. Kitchenbrand leaned forward and felt for his rifle in its scabbard. He was beginning to feel edgy. He had spent many nights alone on the open prairie without having that sensation, but this was something different. The mere presence of the empty deserted buildings lent an extra dimension of solitude; he had the strange notion that their occupiers had only just left. The whole atmosphere was eerie.

They were approaching the outermost shack when Kitchenbrand became aware that they were being watched. It was a kind of sixth sense he had developed over the years and he was seldom mistaken. He wondered if Virginy felt, the same but decided against saying anything to her, even though the hairs on the back of his neck seemed to rise and he felt a tingling sensation run down the back of his head. Every instinct told him to get down from the saddle but something impelled him to ride on. He kept his head facing forward but his eyes swivelled. It was darker down in the valley than it had been on the hillside and once they were among the buildings the shadows were deeper. The wind had died and the only sound was the slow soft thud of their horses' hoofs.

Suddenly he thought he detected a glimmer of something paler than the surrounding gloom on the balcony of what appeared to be a saloon. His nerves were fluttering and it took a conscious effort to hold at bay a rising tide of dread that clutched at his throat and stomach with fingers of ice. He would far rather have faced any number of desperadoes than this unknown phantom.

His eyes caught a faint suggestion of movement. Instinctively he reached for his six-guns. Then he heard a faint moaning sound which for a moment froze the blood in his veins till his senses returned and he realized it was not the moan of a banshee but the faint sound of someone in distress. Virginy's glance indicated that she had heard it too.

In a second he had dropped from the saddle. Quickly he tied his horse to a hitch rail and, as Virginy did likewise, he slipped carefully through the batwing doors. His eyes could discern very little but as they grew accustomed to the darkness he was able to perceive a stairway in one corner. Still moving with extreme caution, he made his way across the intervening space, colliding with some chairs and a table as he did so. He hesitated for a moment when his foot found the bottom stair, before beginning a slow ascent. His gun was in his hand, although he had no recollection of having drawn it. He came to a landing and had to pause again, even though the darkness was not so dense. A soft footfall on the stair behind him made him start till he realized it was Virginy. He put a finger to his lips. A very faint light was entering the passageway from an open door. As he moved towards it he heard again the faint moan. It was

80

coming from inside the room.

When he reached the open door he pressed himself against the wall, his senses strained to gather any information. The moaning sound was repeated. Gathering his courage, he flung himself into the room. He dropped to one knee to take stock and quickly saw that there was another doorway at the opposite end, leading to the balcony; lying across it was a partly clothed figure. He got to his feet and approached it cautiously. When he got close he could see that it was a woman. She was lying face down but when he kneeled and touched her she responded by turning her head. When she saw Kitchenbrand she gasped.

'It's OK,' he said. 'I don't mean you any harm.'

She looked over Kitchenbrand's shoulder and saw the dim figure of Virginy. As far as Kitchenbrand could tell in the shadowy light, there were no obvious signs of injuries. The girl began to struggle and got as far as a sitting position. She cringed away from him, leaning against the door stanchion.

'My name is Kitchenbrand,' he said, 'Hollis Kitchenbrand. This lady is called Virginy.'

She didn't reply but only continued to regard him with a frightened look. He noticed for the first time that her eye was bruised.

'Let me help you to a chair,' he said.

She flinched away when he made to pick her up, but did not offer any further resistance. He took her in his arms and carried her to a settee. He could not help but notice how light and fragile she seemed. When he had laid her down he turned away as she pulled her clothes up around her. They were torn and dirty and there were traces on them of what looked like blood. For an odd moment she reminded him of Virginy when he had first found her.

He looked about him. There was a lamp on a table; he took some matches from his pocket and succeeded in lighting it.

'This place seems to be a saloon,' he said. 'It might be an idea if I went downstairs and got you a drink of brandy.' He moved towards the door but was stopped when the girl suddenly spoke.

'Don't leave me,' she said. 'Just give me a little time.'

Virginy sat beside her and took her hand. 'It's OK,' she said. 'I'll stay with you.'

Kitchenbrand quickly made his way back down the stairs and returned with a bottle of brandy and a glass. He poured some of the liquid and held it out for the girl. She took it and after taking a sip she seemed to gather herself together a little. Nobody spoke for a while. The lamplight seemed to assure her and it was she who eventually broke the silence.

'I haven't seen you before,' she said, addressing Kitchenbrand. 'Maybe you're not one of Addison's men.'

Her words reminded Kitchenbrand of what he was doing there and confirmed his supposition that he had found the Yuma gang's roost.

'No,' he replied. 'You don't need to worry yourself on that score.'

For the first time she looked at him squarely. 'You don't look like any of them,' she added.

Virginy tightened her grip on the girl's hand. 'What's a poor girl like you doin' all alone in this place? You've no need to be frightened. Whatever's happened, you're safe now.'

The girl's face had been turned away; now she looked up at Virginy and for the first time the old lady noticed her bruised eye.

'Lords a' mercy, whatever happened to your eye? I figure that needs bathing. I'll go get some water.' She got up and shuffled from the room. When she had gone the girl turned to Kitchenbrand again.

'You asked me my name,' she said. 'It's Delta, Delta Trace.'

'Only Trace I ever knowed is the Natchez Trace,' Kitchenbrand replied.

There was a flicker of response from the girl. 'It's funny you should say that,' she said. 'You see, that's where I got my name from.'

'Don't you have a proper name?'

'No. I never knew who my parents were. I can just about remember livin' with some nuns and then I guess they musta passed me on. I can recall livin' on the bayou but it weren't long before I was lookin' out for myself.'

Kitchenbrand considered her words. 'So how long have you been here?' he asked.

At his words the girl seemed to shrink away, but just as the situation threatened to grow awkward the sound of footsteps announced the return of Virginy. She came into the room carrying a bowl of water and what looked like a package.

'Comfrey leaves,' she said. 'I always carry a few medicines in my bag. I'll need to boil them in the water.'

Taking his cue, Kitchenbrand volunteered to organize something. He was thinking that in any case they needed to set themselves up for the rest of the night. He made his way back down the stairs and through the empty saloon into the open. The dim shapes of the deserted structures loomed up out of the darkness. The horses nickered, reminding him of their presence. From an open window above him he could hear the muted voices of Virginy and the girl, but he could not distinguish what they were saying.

He looked around. The place seemed to be deserted; only the girl, for whatever reason, had been left behind. Yet, even in the dark, he could see that it was quite an elaborate set-up. Not the sort of place that would be likely to be left empty indefinitely. The girl might have some of the answers. She had obviously suffered at the hands of the Yuma gang. He was chary of upsetting her; maybe Virginy would succeed in putting her at her ease sufficiently for her to provide them with the information about Addison and the Yuma gang that they needed if they were ever to get to the bottom of the affair and find Ty Garland.

★ ★ ★

Landon Clovis ran the biggest ranch in the area, the Latigo, and was well on the way to owning the better part of Chaparral Bend. Anyone who knew Angel Addison would have been surprised, therefore, to see him sitting at a table in the restaurant of the High Pike hotel, deep in conversation with the town's most respected citizen. The High Pike was owned by Clovis. Although Clovis was quite adept at concealing his true feelings, the same observer might have noticed a subdued tension in the atmosphere.

'I ain't in any mood for foolin' about,' Clovis said. 'You tell me you got Garland. I figured somethin' was afoot when I heard the marshal was wounded in some sort of shootin' incident. I take it that was some of your boys?'

By way of reply Addison raised his brows and depressed his mouth, giving a quizzical expression to his face.

'I thought as much,' Clovis said. 'I already warned you about steppin' outa line and takin' things too far. I had to put myself in the front line the night the townsfolk took him in. That was your fault too. You took a big risk robbin' the bank.'

'I figured you'd be pleased about that. I gather Tom Farley was the only man around here who could stand against you.'

'That's beside the point. I coulda dealt with Farley in my own way. And OK, you didn't know the townsfolk were goin' to take against Garland in quite the way they did, but you're a fool if you imagined there'd be no comeback. You could have put all our plans at risk. As it was, I had to guard against any of 'em lynchin' him. But doin' what you did to the old woman was unnecessary.'

Addison's lip curled in an ugly grin.

'That was just some of the boys lettin' off a little steam. They got to have some fun. It ain't no hair off your hide.'

'Don't be stupid,' Clovis replied. 'The more you and your high-line riders indulge in that sort of behaviour, the more likely they are to draw attention not just to themselves but to me as well. I reckon the marshal already has some suspicions.'

'You're the big man around these parts,' Clovis replied. 'Why don't you get rid of him and put your own man in?'

'That's none of your goldurn business. But there's already one consequence of all this; Virginy Garland seems to have acquired some sort of ally.'

'Ally?'

'I hear she's been seen in the company of a man. From what I can gather, he's not been seen around here before but my information is that he looks like a real curly wolf. Now that's just an added complication.'

'Hell, he must be hard up if he's

goin' around with Garland's old grand-mother.'

'Do you have to bring everything down to your level?'

'Even if it's true, what's one man gonna do against all of us?'

'I'd prefer it if you didn't include me with the rest of your gang,' Clovis said. 'It may be the case that our interests so far have run in conjunction, but that don't mean I want to have anything more to do with you than I have to.'

Further conversation was interrupted by the return of the waitress. Addison looked at her with an openly leering expression.

'We're fine,' Clovis said. 'We won't be wantin' anything else.'

She gave an obsequious bob and made her way back across the room.

'Nice,' Addison remarked. 'I figure bein' the big noise in town must have a lot of advantages.'

'You disgust me,' Clovis said. He gave Addison a disdainful glance. 'However, for the moment our fortunes seem to be linked so let me get straight to the point. You got Garland. I want to have a talk with that young man. So what's your askin' price for handin' him over?'

Addison's face twisted into an ugly grin again. 'Now that depends on just how important you think his information is. You ain't told us too much yet about just exactly what it is that Garland knows.'

'That's none of your business.'

'I reckon it became my business the day you hired us on to scare folk into sellin' out to you.'

'Keep your voice down,' Clovis said.

Addison laughed. 'You're gettin' a mite jumpy,' he replied.

'I warn you,' Clovis said. 'You're already close to pushin' things too far.'

Addison stared hard at Clovis before replying. 'OK, let's say ten thousand dollars.'

It was Clovis's turn to laugh, but there was no element of humour in it. 'Don't waste my time,' he said.

'We got Garland. We could make him talk ourselves and find out that way just what he knows.'

Clovis snorted. 'Why don't you do that?' he said. 'See where it gets you.'

'I could start talkin' and blow your whole show,' Addison said.

'You think anyone would take your word over mine? I rather think it's you who should be worried about me spillin' the beans.'

Addison shuffled. He was goaded by Clovis's air of calmness. 'We know somethin' about it already,' he said.

'OK, then go ahead. See if you can get Garland to tell you the rest.' Clovis got to his feet and took a step away from the table.

'All right,' Addison said. 'No need for us to fall out over this. Ten thousand dollars and we'll hand him over.'

'Five thousand,' Clovis said. 'Take it or leave it.'

Addison was ruffled and when he was ruffled he found it hard to think straight. Through his confusion he hung on to one maxim. Let Clovis do the work. He didn't believe that Garland knew anything that would be worth much money. Garland had boasted about a lot of things when he was riding with the Yuma boys. They didn't amount to a hill of beans. But just in case there was a possibility that Garland was not boasting, that he did know something that Clovis wanted, then it made sense to let Clovis do the spadework and then, if it was worth their while, they could step in later to eliminate the rancher and take the rewards for themselves. When he had figured out that plan of action, it had seemed clever. It still did. He had to hang on to it.

'Five thousand now, maybe more later if I get the information I want,' Clovis conceded.

'OK,' Addison said. 'It's a deal. We'll bring Garland over to the ranch later tonight.'

'No. I don't want Garland to suspect that there's any connection between the

Yuma boys and me. There's an old line shack just on the edge of the Latigo spread near the lower ford.'

'I know it,' Addison said.

'Meet me there at sundown. And don't try any tricks. Remember you'll still be on Latigo property and my men will have the place covered.'

'I'll be there with Garland,' Addison said. 'Just make sure you got the money.'

4

Kitchenbrand had been reluctant to wait about the outlaw roost for long because he couldn't be sure if any of the outlaws had been left behind. While Virginy and Delta were still sleeping, before the dawn, he had slipped out of the hotel and made a quick reconnaissance of the settlement. It was enough to satisfy him that the place was indeed completely deserted. The only living things he found were some horses, which had been left in a broken down corral behind one of the buildings on the hillside. Whether they had simply been abandoned or were an indication that the outlaws intended returning soon, he couldn't be sure. If it was the latter it strengthened his inclination to be gone. He was for getting away as quickly as possible, but Virginy assured him that the girl had received a severe shock and there was nothing to be gained by rushing her.

Virginy had found out a little more about her. It seemed she had been the main target of Angel Addison's perverted lusts. The night he rode out she had been subjected to some particularly brutal treatment and there were less obvious injuries than a bruised eye. In such matters Kitchenbrand was more than happy to bow to the old lady's superior knowledge and experience. As the morning slipped by, however, Delta began to feel better and affirmed that she was ready to leave. They stayed long enough to eat and then rode out in the early afternoon.

Kitchenbrand had tried questioning the girl about Addison's plans, but talk of the outlaw leader and his gang only seemed to upset her and it was soon clear to Kitchenbrand that she knew nothing of Addison's intentions. It didn't matter because it was plain to see in which direction the Yuma boys had gone. There was plenty of sign. It was just a question of following it.

It led them through a pass in the hills which seemed to be leading in the opposite direction from that in which Kitchenbrand and Virginy had approached the outlaw roost. After a time, though, it tended in a north-easterly direction and Kitchenbrand gradually began to feel sure that it was leading them back towards Chaparral Bend. If the timing had been different, they might almost have met the outlaws coming along the trail. The only thing that caused Kitchenbrand a little concern was that the sign indicated that fewer riders had been involved than he would have imagined.

'Is there any more to the place you call Addisonville than what we've seen?' he asked Delta.

'No, but I haven't been any further than the settlement.' She paused for a moment. 'But now you mention it, I have seen riders coming and going from different directions.'

'You mean other than the way we've just come?'

'Yes. I think there could be other places they hide out. Maybe not so big. Maybe just a few shacks. I don't know.'

Kitchenbrand reckoned that the sign had been made by only about eight horses, and he concluded that there must be further outlaw hideouts scattered through the hills. Delta's words only confirmed his growing suspicions. It seemed they had been lucky to find the outlaw roost deserted. It was going to take some effort if they were ever to be prised out.

As they got close to town, the tracks they were following divided. As far as he could discern, two riders had continued into Chaparral Bend but the others had taken a side trail.

'Any idea where this might lead?' Kitchenbrand said to Virginy.

'Can't be certain,' she replied, 'but it seems to be goin' in the general direction of the Latigo.'

'Clovis's outfit?' Kitchenbrand said.

Virginy pursed her mouth and then

spat to one side as if at the mention of Clovis's name. 'Yeah. Clovis. But there's other spreads out that way.'

The recurrence of the rancher's name set Kitchenbrand thinking again. Virginy had identified Clovis as being present when the mob had taken Ty Garland. Now what could have been his interest in the matter?

Kitchenbrand and Virginy had considered carrying on into Chaparral Bend and registering Delta at the hotel. However, they had both come to the conclusion that it might not be the wisest thing to do. Virginy's shack was a useful base. It wasn't far from town and it was out of the way. Until things became clearer, it seemed to Kitchenbrand and the old lady that discretion might be advisable. Even at an obvious level, if the girl was seen in town it would make it easy for Addison to trace her if he was so inclined and that could lead to unnecessary complications. Accordingly, they turned off the trail and set their course for the old shack.

★ ★ ★

Ty Garland lay on a bunk in a dark room. He had been pretty well done in when they brought him and he must have slept. He had only a vague idea of how long he had been there. He got to his feet, walked to the door and tried the handle, but he knew it was no use. He had checked the room out carefully when they first locked him in and he knew there was no means of escape. The only thing he could do was to wait till the outlaws returned; at that stage, he might be presented with an opportunity. Could it only have been the previous evening that he had arrived at Addison's roost after being taken from Marshal Purdom's house?

Whatever Addison had in mind for him, it wasn't going to be good. The locked door was a token of that. After his arrival at the robbers' roost, Addison's attitude towards him had been friendly enough but Ty wasn't fooling himself on that score. Addison was capable of extending the hand of friendship while concealing within it a deadly knife. He was not to be trusted and Ty was pretty certain that Addison had his own reason for busting him free.

He didn't know just what that reason was, but of one thing he was certain. He needed to get away somehow. He wondered what had become of the marshal. He was certain that Purdom had been injured and there was a big chance that he would get the blame for it, the same way he had taken the blame for the bank robbery. It wouldn't matter that he had had no choice. Addison and some of his hard-cases had broken into the marshal's house without warning. It would have been better if he had stayed in jail.

He thought about the stranger who had appeared out of the blue. Although Ty couldn't be blamed for what had happened, he felt that he had somehow betrayed the man's trust. All of which made it more incumbent upon him than ever somehow to make his getaway. He would return to Chaparral Bend and try to clear his name whatever the consequences — and they were likely to be grave. Most of the town was against him because of the robbery; the place might still be seething with hostility towards him if people believed he was responsible for what had happened to the marshal. And he was sure that they would feel that way. What would his poor old grandmother make of it all?

* * *

The more Kitchenbrand thought about the situation, the less he liked it. It had seemed the obvious thing to do to follow the gunslicks' trail back to Chaparral Bend, but the more he considered the matter, the less confident he felt. If there were so few riders, what had become of the rest of the outlaws? If they were the ones responsible for wounding the marshal and taking Ty Garland, was it not likely that Garland was still back there in the hills?

He had assumed that the roost he and Virginy had ridden into comprised the whole of the outlaw hideout, but from what Delta had said and what his own instincts told him, there was more to the roost than what they had seen. The Buzzard range was extensive. Behind the hills they had ridden into there were other ranges. The place was out of bounds to anyone except outlaws and desperadoes.

The conclusion seemed to be more and more obvious that the shanty town of shacks, with its false-front saloon, wasn't the outlaws' only retreat. In which case, Ty Garland could still be there, concealed somewhere in the maze of coulees and canyons lying deeper in the wilderness.

If that was true, a further question arose. What were the riders they were following doing? Why had they left the roost and come back in the direction of Chaparral Bend? It would have made more sense for them to make themselves scarce, especially if the bank robbery was taken into account. Why had they taken a back trail which led, according to Virginy, in the direction of the Latigo ranch? Again his thoughts brought him up against the name of Landon Clovis.

Kitchenbrand tried to put his thoughts to one side as they approached Virginy's shack. He had some vague concern that someone might have found the place, but it was exactly as they had left it.

'You worry too much,' Virginy said when he mentioned his concerns.

'Guess that's one reason I manage to stay alive,' he retorted.

He had been apprehensive about how Delta would regard the shack but he needn't have worried. With Virginy's support, she seemed to find herself quite at home. While the women were making themselves comfortable, Kitchenbrand tended to the horses. When he had fed and watered them and given them a rub-down, he set his saddle back on the roan.

'Where are you goin'?' Virginy said.

'Figured I'd ride into town and see how the marshal is,' Kitchenbrand replied.

She nodded. 'I been thinkin' about Purdom myself,' she said.

'You sure you'll be OK here while I'm gone?' he queried.

'Why shouldn't I? You get goin'. Give the marshal my regards.'

Kitchenbrand stepped into leather. When he was close to town he dismounted and hobbled the roan before going the rest of the way on foot. If Addison was in town, he didn't want to advertise his arrival. Quickly he made his way to the marshal's house; when he knocked on the door it was opened by Bella Mayes.

'Don't I know you from some-wheres?' she asked.

'Yeah. Me and the marshal had coffee at the Fashion Restaurant.'

Recognition showed in her face.

'Sure,' she said. 'I remember now. Wasn't that the day the marshal got shot?'

'Yeah. That's what I've come for. To see how he's gettin' on.'

As if in answer to his query there came a shout from inside the house. 'Seems like I recognize that voice. If it's Hollis Kitchenbrand, show him right on in.'

Bella smiled. 'Guess you got your answer,' she said. She motioned for Kitchenbrand to enter. He went into the main room but Purdom wasn't there.

'Out back,' Bella said. 'On the veranda.'

Just at that moment the marshal appeared in the doorway. His head was swathed in a bandage and a lump beneath his shirt indicated he had a compress on his chest, but otherwise he looked in good condition.

'Still takes me a moment or two to get goin',' he said. 'Kitchenbrand, it's sure good to see you.' Kitchenbrand shook his outstretched hand.

'Coffee?' Bella asked.

Before Kitchenbrand could reply, the marshal answered for him. 'I figure our visitor might appreciate somethin' a little stronger,' he said. 'Ain't that right, Kitchenbrand?'

'Whatever you got,' Kitchenbrand replied.

The marshal ushered him to the veranda where two chairs stood next to a table on which stood a half-full bottle of whiskey. Purdom pointed to one chair and sank into the other himself.

'I'll get Mr Kitchenbrand a glass,' Bella said. She turned to him. 'I've tried tellin' him the whiskey ain't what Doc Groves ordered, but he's incorrigible.' She went away and returned after a few moments with a glass and another bottle. 'I'll leave you boys to it,' she said.

When she had gone Purdom poured the whiskey 'This ain't none of your tarantula juice,' he said. 'Best Irish. All the way from St Louis.'

Kitchenbrand took a good sip. 'Yeah, that sure hits the spot,' he said.

He looked out from the veranda over the garden which sloped down to a stream beyond which the land rose towards a line of trees. It was a peaceful scene now. He turned back to Purdom. 'So how are you doin?' he said.

'Doc Groves done a good job and Bella is as good a nurse as a body'd be likely to find. To tell you the truth, I don't think I was hurt too bad.'

'You lost a lot of blood,' Kitchenbrand replied.

'Yeah, maybe so, but the bullet didn't touch nothin' vital. As for the head wound, it ain't the first time I been slugged and it ain't likely to be the last. But what about you, Kitchenbrand? I figured you went after whoever jumped me.'

In as few words as it took to make the story intelligible, Kitchenbrand outlined what had happened since he had left Chaparral Bend. When he had finished, the marshal looked thoughtful.

'So what do you think?' he asked. 'Do you still reckon Garland is innocent, that he didn't know anythin' about all this?'

Kitchenbrand took another swig of the whiskey. 'I don't know,' he said, 'but I still got a leanin' to favour old Virginy.'

Purdom grunted. 'You know somethin'?' he said. 'I figure you could be right. I don't recall anythin' much of the attack, but I got a feelin' that Garland was taken by surprise as much as me.' He paused, trying to remember what had happened, but then shook his head. 'So what do you intend doin' now?' he asked.

'I ain't sure, but I got a hunch that Garland might still be back in those hills.'

'You goin' back?'

'Yup. But I'd like to know what Addison is doin' around Chaparral Bend.'

'Are you sure he's here?'

'If not him, some of his gunnies certainly are.' Kitchenbrand looked again at the marshal. 'Somethin' else,' he said. 'What can you tell me about Landon Clovis?'

The marshal grunted before finishing his drink. He reached for the new bottle and splashed some of it into their glasses. 'Landon Clovis is a big power around these parts,' he said. 'Why do you ask?'

'His name seems to crop up quite often,' Kitchenbrand replied. 'I'm dealin' a lot in hunches, but I got another one that there could be some sort of tie-in between the Yuma gang and Clovis.'

'Funny you should say that. I ain't got nothin' on Clovis, but I don't like him. He seems to get his way a mite too often. I've had my suspicions about him too, but he's clever, clever enough not to get himself in trouble with the law.'

'Maybe for once he's got too clever,' Kitchenbrand said.

They lapsed into silence till eventually Purdom spoke again. 'Do you intend stayin' in town for long?'

'Nope,' Kitchenbrand replied. He

hadn't given it much thought.

'You're welcome to stay here.'

'Thanks for the offer, but Virginy and the girl will be expectin' me back.' He got to his feet. 'Glad to see you lookin' so good,' he said. 'That whiskey sure seems to be doin' the trick.'

'I figure I'm almost right,' Purdom said. He seemed about to elaborate but instead got to his feet to accompany Kitchenbrand to the front door.

Bella appeared from the kitchen. 'You're goin' already?' she asked.

'Mr Kitchenbrand has some business in town,' Purdom said.

As he walked away, Kitchenbrand looked back at the pair of them framed in the doorway of the house. Evening was drawing down and his intention was to return immediately to the shack, but something Purdom had said made him resolve to go back the next morning. Maybe he could flush out some information, even just a rumour, in Chaparral Bend before heading out to pay another visit to the outlaw roost.

It seemed an age to Ty Garland that he had been standing behind the door of the room in which he was imprisoned, waiting for the arrival of his captors. He had almost given up hope when he heard the sound of boots scraping the floor and then the jingling of keys. The moment that the door swung open he launched himself upon the first person who entered the room. The man was pushed back and Garland landed on top of him, bringing his fist down with a crash into the man's face. As he swung his arm up to deliver a second blow someone seized it and then another arm was round his neck, pulling him back and closing so tight that he began to choke. He felt a boot thud into his stomach and then a black sickness surged up and overwhelmed him.

He could only have been unconscious for a few moments because when he came round he was kneeling on the floor surrounded by four pairs of legs. He looked up into the leering face of Angel Addison. Next to him a mean-faced man was holding a blood soaked rag to his nose.

'Now that just weren't friendly,' Addison sneered.

'Go to hell, Addison!' Garland muttered. He didn't want to let Addison and his henchmen see how hurt he was, but he couldn't avoid a groan escaping from him.

'Is that any way to talk to an old partner?' Addison said.

'You were never no partner of mine.'

'That's not the way I remember it. Time was you were proud to ride with the Yuma gang.' Garland did not reply. His stomach was hurting and he felt sick.

'I think you owe Cord an apology,' Addison said. The injured man held the kerchief away from his face. His nose was split and badly mashed.

'Go to hell!' Garland repeated.

Before he had an inkling that it was

about to happen, Cord's boot slammed into his jaw. He fell to one side, spitting blood and teeth, as the heel of Cord's boot came down between his shoulders. Cord was about to deliver more punishment when Addison held out his arm to stop him.

'That'll do for now,' he said. 'I think he's got the message. Besides, Clovis is goin' to want him still in one piece.' He looked down at the writhing figure of Garland. 'Take that as a warning,' he said. 'We're gonna be takin' a ride. I'd advise you not to try anythin' like that again.'

At a nod from Addison, the other two desperadoes bent down, seized Garland, and hauled him to his feet. Barely conscious of what was happening to him, Garland was led through another sparsely furnished room and then out of the building.

A freshening wind blowing down from the mountains came like a douse of water, reviving Garland sufficiently for him to be able to take some interest in his surroundings. He was in a part of the hills he did not recognize. It certainly wasn't the settlement Addison liked to call Addisonville. During his time with the Yuma gang, Garland had spent time in various outlaw fastnesses, but he was sure that this was not one of them.

Another of the outlaws was standing with six horses. Ignoring Garland's pain and discomfort, the two outlaws who had dragged him to his feet proceeded to haul him unceremoniously on to the back of one horse. The others mounted and they set off, one of them leading Garland's horse while the others closed around him. The movement of the horse was agony to Garland in his damaged condition, and as they rode he began to retch. The others took no notice. Addison's flippant mood seemed to have deserted him. Once he had been sick Garland gradually began to feel a little better. He tried to take cognizance of his surroundings and the route they were following. He observed his captors more carefully.

'Where are we goin'?' he said.

There was no response from the people on either side of him. He leaned forward and shouted to Addison, repeating his question, but with the same result. As time passed and he felt better, he began once again to look for an opportunity to escape.

★   ★   ★

Following the decision he had made the previous evening, Hollis Kitchenbrand rode into Chaparral Bend. As he passed beneath the gallows he observed that it was completed. The townsfolk didn't seem to be wasting any time. On this occasion he did not leave the roan behind but carried on till he reached the saloon, where he dismounted and tied it to the hitch-rack. He wasn't bothered whether or not anyone recognized him because he had a feeling that if someone did, it might in fact serve his purposes. It might act as some sort of catalyst.

He stepped up on the boardwalk and brushed his way through the batwing doors. Although it was still early, a number of people were sitting around the tables and a small group of men had gathered at the bar. They wore guns slung low. Kitchenbrand recalled the marshal telling him that guns were not allowed in town. One of the men carried his arm in a sling.

Kitchenbrand's thoughts flashed back to the sniper who had bushwhacked him at Virginy's wrecked house. It wasn't these indications that told him the men belonged to the Yuma boys. Something about the way they stood and their grim faces in the bar mirror was sufficient to indicate that they were no ordinary cowboys. The man with the sling glanced up as he approached the bar. It seemed to Kitchenbrand that the recognition was mutual.

'What's it to be?' the bartender said.

He seemed nervous. Kitchenbrand placed his boot heel on the brass rail.

'Bourbon.'

The bartender splashed the liquor into a glass and was about to move away when Kitchenbrand put a hand on his arm.

'Leave the bottle,' he said. He turned to the man with his arm in a sling. 'Maybe you and your friends would care to join me?'

The man glanced at his two companions. 'We got a drink,' one of them said.

'Sure.' Kitchenbrand tossed back the glass and poured another. Behind him, reflected in the mirror, he saw another couple of men enter the saloon. They were carrying guns too. Some of the people at the tables were looking anxiously around and one man near the batwings got to his feet and made a quick exit.

'I just figured you boys might need to build up a little courage,' Kitchenbrand remarked. The man who had spoken stepped away from the bar and faced him.

'What do you mean by that?' he said.

Kitchenbrand took another drink. The bourbon was strong and burned its way down his throat. He knew how much he could take before it might begin to affect him, and he figured the Yuma boys had been drinking for some time before he entered the saloon. He turned sideways to look at his interlocutor.

'Well, I figure it takes some courage for you boys to face up to a woman,' he replied. 'I figure you're gonna need somethin' to stiffen you up the next time you decide to tar and feather an old lady.'

The man's face twisted into an ugly snarl. 'Why, you — ' he began.

His hand dropped to his holster but Kitchenbrand's cross-draw was too quick for him. Before his gun was in his hand, Kitchenbrand's bullet tore into his chest and sent him crashing against the bar. As the second owlhoot went for his gun, Kitchenbrand spun and fired again. The man staggered back as two slugs smashed into him and then he dropped to the sawdust like a felled log.

At the same instant a shot rang out from the back of the saloon. If Kitchenbrand hadn't moved, the bullet would have caught him full on. As it was it went whistling just past him, shattering the bar mirror. Kitchenbrand flung himself sideways and dropped to the floor as more slugs went ricocheting around the room. He was looking for the two men who had come through the batwing doors but he couldn't see them for gunsmoke and the haze of tobacco which hung over the room like a shroud.

A bullet thudded into the floor next to him and he had just realized that the next one would probably find its mark when the batwings flew open and someone burst into the room, opening fire as he did so.

A voice screamed. Kitchenbrand saw one of the owlhoots stagger back. He looked to the other side of the room where the fourth gunman was bent low in a corner, pumping lead. He raised his gun and fired at the same time as the newcomer; both bullets found their target. The man fell forward, firing one more slug harmlessly into the floor, and then lay still.

Silence suddenly fell. The whole incident had taken only a matter of seconds but it seemed to Kitchenbrand that a long time had passed. He became aware that the man with his arm in a sling was crouched under the bar and making a strange whimpering sound. He looked towards the batwings; only then did he recognize the newcomer as Marshal Purdom. The marshal stepped forward as Kitchenbrand got back to his feet.

'Are you OK, Kitchenbrand?' the marshal asked.

Kitchenbrand was too surprised to answer directly. 'Purdom!' he snapped. 'What in hell are you doin' here?'

Purdom didn't reply. Instead he went over to look at the bodies of the four outlaws to confirm that they were dead.

'Someone go and get the undertaker,' he said.

The rest of the clientele were just beginning to recover their wits and were looking about them at the scene of carnage with shocked expressions. Purdom approached the bar and, bending down, seized the man with his arm in a sling and dragged him to his feet.

'You and I got some talkin' to do later,' he said. 'In the jailhouse.' He turned to Kitchenbrand. 'You said you'd be comin' back to town. Somehow I kinda figured there might be trouble. I saw your horse outside the saloon. Looks like I got here just in time.'

'Sure appreciate it,' Kitchenbrand replied. 'Without your assistance, I figure those two galoots mighta got me. But shouldn't you be restin' up?'

'Bella's a marvellous woman. She's been doin' a great job takin' care of me, but I couldn't take no more sittin' about. I was startin' to go plumb loco. Besides, you didn't think I was gonna let you ride out to the Buzzards all by yourself? You might be good, but it's a tall order even for you, takin' on a bunch of renegades like the Yuma gang in their own hideout.'

'I figure I could handle 'em.'

'Maybe so. You made a good start right here. But I figure there's plenty more of 'em roostin' up there.' He turned to the injured outlaw. 'I think you've got a lot of explainin' to do, and we're gonna find it mighty interestin'.'

★　★　★

As he rode in the midst of his captors, Ty Garland continued to look for an opportunity to escape. He had just about given up hope when suddenly he saw his chance. It was a desperate one, but he could think of nothing else. The track they were following led along the side of a hill. Below them ran a mountain stream. If he could get closer to the edge of the trail, he might be able to leap from the saddle. It was a long drop and he had no way of knowing how deep the water was. If there had been rain or even snow higher in the mountains, it might have swelled the current, but it was still an awful risk.

He looked ahead along the trail. The particular section they were following was fairly level. The outlaw leading his horse seemed to have relaxed his hold on the rope. There was another outlaw between him and the edge of the trail. Very stealthily he tried to edge slightly towards him. The trail was quite narrow and there wasn't much room for manoeuvre. He glanced downwards out of the corner of his eyes once again at the river and almost lost his nerve. Now that he was about to put his plan into effect, it seemed an even greater drop. Another question was whether he would be able to project himself far enough to avoid hitting the cliff face.

He looked away again, swallowed hard and took some deep breaths to try and steady himself. Then, gathering his courage into one tight ball, he suddenly dug his heels into the horse's flanks.

It started forward and sideways, colliding with the horse on the outside. For a moment he had a glimpse of the look of horror on its rider's face as his horse reared and then slipped. In the same moment that the outlaw's horse lost its footing and went over the edge, braying in terror, Garland launched himself from the saddle and followed the doomed horse and rider into the abyss.

He seemed to be falling for a long time and then something hit him like a blackjack across his shoulders, leaving him gasping for breath as he sank beneath the water. Panic swept over him as he began frantically to kick and thresh in an effort to stop his descent and move upwards. He was totally disoriented, so it came as a shock when his head burst through the surface of the water and light burst around him in an exploding rainbow.

He began to move his arms and legs, swimming blindly but gradually becoming aware of his situation. Something fizzed into the water not far from his head and he realized he was being shot at from the top of the hillside. Reacting quickly, he took a deep breath and ducked his head. He swam under water towards the cliff face, thinking that he might gain some protection from the overhang. The water on that side was shadowed and he would be less visible. He popped his head out of the water to take another gulp of air and then continued swimming. He was feeling very tired and he ached all over but he carried on, summoning up every ounce of energy and determination he still possessed. The water was murky and he kept his eyes shut so long as he was beneath the surface.

Suddenly he felt something seize his foot and panic gripped him as he realized it was caught in some kind of trailing root or weed. He pulled hard and to his relief his foot came away from the entanglement. Opening his eyes, he saw the riverbed and realized that the river was becoming shallower. He feared that he might be left stranded, an easy target for Addison and his men above, but as if to compensate the current began to speed up. He surfaced once more and, lying on his back in order to conserve what little strength he still possessed, allowed the current to carry him onwards.

Soon he was going at quite a quick rate but the water remained a lot shallower and some rocks and other obstructions were appearing in the water. Turning his head, he saw a large dark object looming up ahead of him. He was in danger of striking it and he kicked out, swerving away. As he passed close by he realized it was the body of the horse which had fallen over the edge of the trail. He could see no sign of its rider.

The river took a wide bend and the current began to slow again. Garland reckoned he had travelled a fair distance down the river away from his captors and was confident that he had made good his escape. Kicking out once more, he began to move towards the opposite shore where stands of cottonwood and willow lined the banks. The river wasn't very wide; soon his feet touched bottom and he was able to stand and wade through the water the rest of the way. Feeling completely exhausted, he flung himself down in the shelter of a tree.

5

When Kitchenbrand got back to the shack and told Virginy what had happened in town he was rewarded by the biggest grin he had ever seen spreading on a face without cracking it.

'Landogoshen!' she said, 'I wish I'd been there to take part. Only pity is that the varmint who tried to shoot you didn't wind up in boot hill with the rest of 'em.'

'Marshal Purdom's got him in jail. He'll get his due deserts.'

Kitchenbrand was about to say something further when their conversation was interrupted by a loud squawk and a cry from inside the shack. In a moment Delta came running out with a bird sitting on her head.

'Don't be frightened,' Virginy called. 'Like I said, she won't hurt you. Lords a' mercy, she's just bein' plumb friendly.'

Fortunately, just at that moment the bird gave another squawk, flew up from the frightened girl's head, and landed on Kitchenbrand's shoulder.

'Goldurnit!' Kitchenbrand said. 'It's Reba! How did she get here?'

'You remembered her name,' Virginy replied. 'And she remembers you.'

Kitchenbrand looked at Delta and they both looked at Virginy. Suddenly the girl began to laugh.

'Now that's better,' Virginy said. 'A pretty young thing like you didn't ought to be all sad and beaten down. That's the first time I seen you smile since we found you.' Kitchenbrand glanced sideways at the crow's glistening eye. 'Reba knows where to find me,' Virginy said. 'She brung me somethin', too.'

She went into the shack and returned carrying a small brooch which she handed to the girl. 'Here, why don't you have it?' she said.

Delta took it and looked at it. It was a plain silver brooch and not especially remarkable, but she obviously liked it. 'I couldn't take it, it's yours,' she replied.

'Shucks, it ain't no use to me now, but it would surely look purty fixed to your blouse.'

After a moment's hesitation Delta did as the old woman suggested.

'Sure does look nice,' Kitchenbrand said.

'Thanks, Virginy. But are you quite sure?'

'Sure as sure. It's a long time since I wore it. I'd forgotten all about it. It does an old lady good to see it bein' put to proper use again. I guess Reba musta flown down one time and taken it. Years ago I remember havin' to check out one of the old rafters in the barn. There were beads and coins up there and pieces of broken glass. She's got an eye for shiny things.'

'Well, she can't be accused of thievin' if she brought it back again,' Kitchen-brand commented.

Further discussion of Reba was ended when the bird suddenly flapped its wings and soared up to the branches of one of the trees overlooking the shack.

★　★　★

Later that same day, Kitchenbrand and Marshal Purdom set off in their quest to find Ty Garland.

They rode hard to reach the Buzzard ranges without further delay. Purdom had questioned the wounded gunslick but hadn't been able to learn a lot that Kitchenbrand didn't already know. The outlaw confirmed that it was the Yuma boys who had tarred and feathered Virginy and torn down her house. It seemed that they had done it simply for the hell of it and he had no idea what Addison's motives were. He knew nothing about the whereabouts of either Addison or Garland. It seemed he was a bit player.

'If I figure Virginy Garland right,' the marshal said, 'I reckon she took some persuadin' not to ride along with us.'

Kitchenbrand nodded. 'Yeah, you're

right,' he said. 'You know, Virginy's quite a lady. I think I persuaded her to see how the two of us might do better without havin' her along, but what really made her stay behind was her concern for Delta.'

'The young lady you were tellin' me about?'

'Yes. They seem to be gettin' along real well.'

'Maybe lookin' after the girl helps her to cope with not knowin' what's happened to her grandson.'

'You could be right.'

Kitchenbrand and Purdom exchanged glances. 'I guess that's all the more reason we got to find him,' Purdom said.

★　★　★

Before Angel Addison had fully realized what had happened, his remaining companions had seized their rifles and were firing into the water.

'Stop that!' Addison yelled. 'Garland ain't no use to us dead!'

'He's probably dead anyway,' one of the others replied. 'That was probably his body we saw.'

Addison leaped off his horse and peered over the edge of the cliff. 'I don't see him,' he said.

'Look! Down there. Hell, he's survived the fall. He's swimmin'.'

Addison examined the side of the hill, considering whether there was any chance of climbing down, but decided it would be too dangerous. 'Quick!' he said. 'We can cut him off further along the trail.'

Two of the gunnies hung back. 'What about McNab?' one of them said.

'What about him!' Addison yelled. 'He couldn't have survived. He must be dead. And if he isn't, our best chance of finding him is by getting on down the trail.'

They stepped into leather and began to move along the track as quickly as they dared. Addison was cursing the others but even in his rage he could see that he was as much to blame as the rest of them. The path began to rise and they made slower progress. It turned away from the river which, for a while, they lost sight of till they came out on a ridge and could see it again, winding away to their right. They rode along the ridge which began to descend gradually towards the river.

As they continued riding Addison brought out a pair of field glasses and put them to his eyes, but he could see no sign of Garland. He was thinking rapidly. Assuming Garland was still alive, which he thought was probable, he wouldn't be able to get far. He was in a bad way and he had no horse, no weapon, and no provisions. He doubted that Garland knew this part of the country. It was wild and rugged and he would find it very hard to make any sort of progress. If he could get more of his men on the job scouring the country to find him, it would greatly increase his chances of finding Garland. He had to get word to the rest of his gang to start looking for him.

'Staines!' he shouted. The gunnie rode up alongside. 'I want you to go back and round up some of the boys. Spread out and start searchin' for Garland. We'll carry on this way.'

'What do we do if we find him?'

Addison was feeling exasperated. 'Never mind about that,' he said. Staines was about to ride off when he added: 'Take him to Addisonville. We'll meet back there.'

Staines turned his horse and began to ride back the way they had come. Addison was thinking that they had better find Garland pretty quick if he was to make the meeting with Clovis.

★ ★ ★

Kitchenbrand had not known what to expect when he and Purdom arrived at the robber roost at Addisonville. Would it still be deserted or would some of the outlaws have returned? In case, he and the marshal took just as much care to avoid being spotted by any possible guards as he had done previously. When they were close he took out his binoculars and took a long, hard look. As far as he could see the place seemed to be empty. There was no sign of any activity. He handed the glasses for Purdom to take a look.

'There's nothin' happenin',' Purdom said. 'So what do we do? Ride on in and see if Garland is there?'

Kitchenbrand gave the matter a moment's thought, then shook his head. 'Nope. If I'm anyways right about this, I still figure they got him hidden someplace else further back in the hills.'

Purdom looked out over the ranges and up to the sweep of mountains beyond.

'It's a big country,' he said. 'It'll be like lookin' for a needle in a haystack.'

'They won't have taken him too far away. Just a bit further than this.'

'Better get ridin' then,' Purdom said. He made to move but Kitchenbrand remained motionless. Purdom looked at him. There was a grim smile on

Kitchenbrand's face.

'I figure we got one little job to do before we move on,' he said.

'Yeah? What's that?'

'We do to that nest of varmints what Addison did to Virginy. We tear the place down.'

Purdom pondered his words for a moment, then his face too lit up in a broad grin.

'What are we waitin' for?' he almost shouted.

They rode down the long slope leading to the collection of wooden huts and dilapidated false fronts. Outside the saloon where Kitchenbrand had found Delta, they brought their horses to a halt.

'Bring your rope,' Kitchenbrand said. He leaped from the saddle, took his own rope and tied it to a stanchion. Purdom followed suit.

'Let's see what those horses can do,' Kitchenbrand said. They climbed into leather. 'OK, pull!' Kitchenbrand shouted.

They spurred their horses and they

moved quickly forward. The ropes stretched taut and for a few moments it looked as if the building might hold as the horses continued to strain. Then, suddenly, there was a noise like a whipcrack; the stanchions snapped and the building sagged. The horses lurched forward and with a tremendous noise of crashing timber the saloon collapsed like a stack of cards. There was a gust of wind and dust rose into the air in a dense cloud. Kitchenbrand looked behind him and Purdom whooped.

'The whole place is rotten,' Kitchenbrand said. 'It didn't take very much.'

'Man, let's do it again,' Purdom shouted.

They dismounted and, pulling up their neckerchiefs as a protection from the dust, undid the ropes and then attached them to the next structure. This time the building lasted for even less time than the saloon. The horses strained; the building leaned forward and then toppled as if it had been a drunken cowhand left behind after a night on the prod.

After another few buildings had been demolished the same way, Kitchenbrand looked about him at the remaining structures and at the other shacks above them on the hillside.

'Much as I'm enjoyin' this, we ain't got time to do 'em all this way,' he said. 'Let's torch the rest of 'em.'

Purdom was on a high. 'Those Yuma boys ain't gonna like this one bit!' he yelled.

Kitchenbrand laughed out loud.

'They'd better have some other places back in the hills because as sure as hell, by the time we've finished, they ain't gonna be usin' this one again,' he replied.

The wooden buildings were dry and it was easy to set them ablaze. As Kitchenbrand and Purdom moved up the hillside, flames began to writhe and pillars of fire soared into the sky. Smoke billowed across the valley as the conflagration crackled and roared. One of the last buildings to be set alight was the larger shack that Addison had been using as his headquarters.

Kitchenbrand did not stop to look into any of the buildings. He was not concerned with what they might contain or whether a search of them might provide useful information about the doings of the Yuma gang, or even clues to the whereabouts of Ty Garland. Both he and Purdom were caught in a fury of destruction. The Yuma gang were going to be made to pay for what they had done, and the two men didn't intend to show any restraint. When at last they were satisfied that all the buildings that were accessible had been set alight, they stopped to watch the inferno.

'Addison figured he was safe up here,' Kitchenbrand said. 'He even called the place after himself. He never bothered to leave some of his boys in charge.'

'There's a word for that kind of attitude,' the marshal said.

'Yeah. They call it *hubris*.'

The marshal shot him a quizzical

glance. 'You ain't just a man with a reputation for a fast gun,' he said.

'They got a word for this too,' Kitchenbrand replied, throwing out his arm to encompass the entire lurid scene. 'They call it *nemesis.*'

Purdom's gaze swept across the burning outlaw roost. 'Like I say, Addison ain't gonna like this one little bit,' he said. 'We still got a lot of work to do. And we still gotta find Ty Garland.'

They watched for a while longer. Then, turning their backs on the conflagration, they climbed into leather and rode away, taking a side trail which seemed to lead them in the direction they wanted to follow. At first it was hard going but after a time it led into a high bowl from which they had a good view of the surrounding country. Behind them, smoke drifted into the air from the ashes of Addisonville. The view was deceptive. Looking about from the edge of the hollow, it was hard to believe that the nearby hills and valleys could conceal a whole rookery of outlaws nests. They sat their horses and observed the scene.

'Which way now?' Purdom eventually asked.

'Towards those higher hills. If there's any outlaws hidin' out round here, that's where they're most likely to be.'

'What about guards? If there's another nest of the varmints, they're likely to have it covered.'

'They didn't back there. Still, I guess we'll have to be careful and just take our chances.'

Purdom looked at Kitchenbrand. 'Sounds like you thought about this real careful,' he said. He grinned. 'Let's hope it all works out better than your last plan to hide Garland.'

★ ★ ★

Virginy Garland shuffled from the kitchen with a bowl of soup in her hands. Delta Trace, sitting at the table, looked up at her approach.

'Here,' Viginy said, 'you need to eat somethin'. Lords a' mercy, you don't put enough away as would keep old Reba satisfied.' She placed the bowl on the table and sat down beside the girl.

'What about you?' Delta said. 'Don't you need to eat too?'

'I'm an old widder woman. I don't need no more to keep me goin' than a crow.'

Delta smiled, took a spoon, and ladled some of the soup into her mouth. Then she looked at the old woman. 'You're a widow?' she said. 'I never thought — '

'You ain't hardly had time to think,' Virginy interrupted her.

Delta drank some more of the soup. 'How long have you been a widow?' she asked. 'If you don't mind me askin'?'

The old lady smiled. 'Mind? Why should I mind?'

'I don't know. I hardly know you. Maybe you'd think it was a little impertinent of me.'

'I don't think that at all. You and me, we get on. I don't mind talkin' about things. Landogoshen, it ain't as if I get much chance these days.' She paused for a moment before continuing. 'His name was Abel, Abel Garland. He were an ornery, hard-cussin' kind of man. Not everyone took to him. But he was a good man. I guess it took one just like him to see it. He was always good with Walt. That's Ty's father.'

She stopped, thinking about what she had just said. 'Ty's a good boy too. I know he got caught up with those Yuma boys. But people can go off the rails. Especially young'uns. He saw where he had gone wrong.'

'I know,' the girl responded. 'Look at what happened to me.'

Virginy looked at her and smiled. She hesitated before going on. 'You're out of all that too, now,' she said.

'I wish I could tell you somethin' about your grandson,' Delta replied. 'But I wasn't with them for long. Ty must have left before I was ever foolish enough to get involved with Angel Addison.'

'It's all right. And if anyone can find him, it's Kitchenbrand. I can tell that he's a good man too.'

They lapsed into silence for a few moments before Delta spoke again. 'I hardly know Mr Kitchenbrand. Sometimes he seems kind of withdrawn, but at the same time I feel comfortable with him around.'

Virginy opened her mouth as if to speak but closed it again. She licked her lips. 'You're a bit young to remember about the War,' she said. 'Mr Kitchenbrand told me he'd been right through it. I think it wounded him.'

'You mean he got shot? He seems to be OK.'

'Not shot. I didn't mean that. But a person can get hurt in other ways.'

Delta thought about it. 'I know what you mean,' she said. 'I know that too.'

Virginy regarded her closely. 'Yes, I think you do,' she said.

When the girl had finished her soup Virginy got to her feet to take the empty bowl back to the kitchen. She was gone for a while and Delta was wondering what had delayed her when she reappeared.

'You didn't say what happened to your son,' Delta said. 'If you're sure you don't mind talkin' about it'

Virginy gently shook her head. 'No, I don't mind,' she replied. 'Walt was wounded, physically wounded I mean. I went to visit him in the hospital. They thought he might pull through, but he didn't quite make it.'

'I'm sorry,' Delta said. 'I shouldn't . . . '

'Don't be silly,' Virginy said. 'I wasn't the only one to lose somebody. After all, like I once said to Mr Kitchenbrand, it was a long time ago now. A lot of things have happened since.' She got to her feet and walked to the window where she stood looking out for a moment or two. 'Now, why don't you and I go for a little walk?' she said. 'It's turning into a lovely evening.'

They got to their feet and walked outside. Before stepping down from the rickety porch Delta stopped Virginy by touching her on the arm. 'I know how worried you must be about your grandson,' she said, 'and I sure appreciate all you're doin' for me. But I'm fine now. We don't have to stay here.'

'What are you drivin' at?' Virginy said.

'You and Mr Kitchenbrand and the marshal ain't the only ones with a grievance against Angel Addison. I got reasons for wantin' to see him brought to justice. Why don't we follow Mr Kitchenbrand and the marshal and ride for the Buzzards?'

Virginy's expression registered her conflicting emotions. 'You mean that?' she said. 'You're sure you're strong enough after all you've been through?'

'I wasn't always like I was when you found me. I can look after myself. Yes, I mean it. I'm ready and what's more, I'm willin' and able to face up to Addison and the rest of those varmints. Mr Kitchenbrand and the marshal might be able to use a little help.'

A new look of relief and eagerness spread across Virginy's countenance.

'If you're sure,' she replied. 'You needed someone to take care of you, but I got to admit I been strainin' at the bit. Lords a' mercy, let's do it. We can pick up what we need in town first thing tomorrow.'

★　★　★

Ty Garland lay for a long time, not moving, not even thinking, lost in some twilight world between sleep and waking, between consciousness and oblivion. When he came round the sun was low in the sky. He ached all over and he was shivering, even though his clothes had dried out in the sun. Slowly, he eased himself to a sitting posture and then got shakily to his feet. A strong breeze rustled in the treetops and sent little choppy waves scurrying across the surface of the water. He looked up at the hillside on the opposite side but there was no sign of Addison and his gang. He knew, however, that they would be after him. They were ruthless and would not stop till they had found him.

At first he had been confused about the whole affair, from the moment he had heard the necktie party causing trouble outside the jailhouse till he had been removed from the marshal's house and taken to Addison. Now, after giving the matter more thought, he had a pretty shrewd idea what it was all about. He was pretty sure he knew what Addison was after.

When he had ridden with the gang and had foolishly considered Addison to be his friend, in moments when his tongue had been loosened by liquor, he had indiscreetly hinted at having the plans to a disused mine on his grandmother's property. There was indeed a document of some sort which his grandmother had once mentioned, but he had never looked into the matter in any detail. Now it seemed that Addison had renewed his interest.

What he couldn't work out was why Addison should do so at this stage and what use a disused mine could be to him even if it existed. Working on some old diggings did not seem to be his style. Something like that was far more likely to interest a man like Landon Clovis, who was growing ever more influential in Chaparral Bend; a man who had a finger in various pies and who had coveted his grandmother's small piece of property for some time.

He recalled the night that the mob of angry townsfolk had come to take him away. He hadn't given it any thought at the time, but could there be any significance in the fact that Clovis had been one of them? Maybe that gold mine was more Ty's own fantasy than he had allowed for. But he guessed the document was real, even though his grandmother had probably forgotten about it. Whatever it contained, it was probably the clue to the mystery.

Right now he needed to do something about his situation, and quickly.

His most pressing needs were for shelter, warmth and dry clothes. He did not feel hungry, but he knew that would come. He walked to the river's edge, stooped down and drank. When he had slaked his thirst, he got to his feet and walked back amongst the trees. He kept on moving till he reached the edge of the tree line, behind which the hills sloped upwards in a gentle incline. A little higher up they became steeper and just at that point his eyes detected openings into what must be caves. His heart skipped. There was the answer to his most immediate problem. Choosing an appropriate spot, he began to climb the hillside.

Although it wasn't especially steep, he found it hard going and by the time he reached the opening he was aiming for and flung himself down on the floor, he was feeling exhausted again. Darkness was drawing down as the sun's last rays struck the hillside and filtered into the cavern.

His refuge didn't extend very far

back. He sat in the entrance and watched the sun drop at last behind the western mountains. The wind freshened up and the trees below swayed. Beyond the river the hills were a black wedge sharply outlined against the sky. He continued to survey the scene and, just as he was about to turn away, his eyes, grown used to the dim light, detected movement along the river away to his right. He was suddenly alert, straining his sight.

For a moment he thought he must be mistaken, when he saw it again. Something was moving on the opposite bank of the river. It got closer and then he saw a couple of riders coining his way. It seemed Addison was close to finding him already.

Instinctively, he shrank back inside the cave. It didn't seem possible that Addison could have tracked him down so quickly. The best thing would be to remain where he was. Surely there was no chance that Addison could discover his exact whereabouts. It had to be down to luck that he had got this far.

Once he had got over the shock of seeing the riders he moved to the front of the cave again to take another look. Moonshine flooded the landscape and he could see well but there was no sign of the riders. Thinking they might have crossed the river, he looked up at the opposite shore, but there was no movement there either. He wasn't sure what to make of it when he heard something almost directly below him. The night was still and sounds carried; he could hear the ripple of the river. He tensed as the sound was repeated.

There was no mistaking the soft thud of horses' hoofs on damp earth. The next moment the two riders emerged from the trees. His heart thumped. If they had been able to follow his trail this far, there was little chance that they would miss the cave where he was hiding. Or maybe it was still just chance that had brought them so close. He peered out once more.

The two riders had stopped and were

talking together. Their voices floated up to him but he could not make out what they were saying. Then the moonlight glanced off some object on the chest of one of the riders and Garland's heart skipped again. It looked like a badge, a star. He squinted, trying to make out the features of the men. Neither of them looked like Addison. Then he started to his feet. The two riders were Marshal Purdom and the stranger he had met in the jailhouse: Kitchenbrand. For a moment he hesitated, uncertain that he had got it right. He continued to look closely at the two men. He was not mistaken; it was Purdom and Kitchenbrand.

He was about to make his presence known when a new thought struck him. What would their attitude be? If they thought he had been involved in the breakout from the marshal's house, it might not be too welcoming. Was that what they were doing here? Had they tracked him down in order to drag him back for the hanging? Their presence could be no coincidence.

Then he thought of the alternative. He couldn't last long in the wilderness in his current state and sooner or later Addison would find him. The fact was that he had been abducted against his will. What had happened was none of his doing. He decided that his best course of action would be to throw himself on the mercy of the marshal and hope that Purdom would believe his side of the story. Stepping out of cover, he waved his arms and called to the riders below.

'Marshal Purdom, Kitchenbrand! It's me, Ty Garland.'

The riders looked up. Garland saw Kitchenbrand reach for his rifle but then stop. The two men exchanged glances.

'Garland! We've been lookin' for you!'

'I guess you found me!' Garland called back.

It didn't take long for Kitchenbrand and the marshal to build a fire in the mouth of the cave and have bacon and beans sizzling in the pan while Garland warmed himself at the flames. He had been apprehensive about the reception he would be given, but Kitchenbrand and the marshal had soon set him at ease. It seemed they were at least willing to listen to his account of events. When they had eaten and filled their cups with strong black coffee, they built smokes and settled back.

'Guess you'd better tell us what this is all about,' Purdom said. 'And you'd better be tellin' it straight.'

When Garland had finished, the marshal looked towards Kitchenbrand. 'Do you believe what he says?' he asked.

Kitchenbrand nodded. 'I believed old Virginy all along,' he said. 'I ain't gonna change my mind about Garland now.'

'How is my grandmother?' Garland said.

'She's fine. She sure is a plucky old girl.'

When Kitchenbrand mentioned the

destruction of Virginy's house, Garland was angry but he calmed down somewhat when Kitchenbrand told him how they had destroyed the outlaw settlement in return.

'I gotta get even on the rest of those coyotes,' Garland said when Kitchenbrand had finished.

'I think we're with you there,' Kicthenbrand said. 'We figure there's some other hole in the wall around here where they're hidin' out. Do you know where it might be and do you reckon you could find your way there?'

Garland thought for a moment. 'There's a lot of old trails and I hardly know the hills, but if I get back to Addisonville and start from there, I reckon I might be able to figure somethin' out.'

'That's good,' Purdom said. 'How are you feelin' now? Do you reckon you'll be up to ridin' in the mornin'?'

'I ain't got a horse.'

'That isn't a problem. There are some horses in a corral back at

Addisonville. You can ride with me and pick one up there.'

They relaxed and enjoyed the coffee and tobacco. Eventually Kitchenbrand spoke again.

'From what we know now, it seems that Addison has been workin' in cahoots with Landon Clovis. Seems like we might have him to deal with as well as Addison. But what I don't understand is what interest either of them would have in your grandmother's property.'

'I think I got a good idea what that is,' Garland said. He proceeded to tell them about the rumour of a disused mine which he had put about.

'You ever come across anythin' like that?' Marshal Purdom asked when he had finished.

'Nope. Grandmother don't know nothin' about it either. I guess I went a bit too far with that gold mine yarn. It was her tellin' me about that document that the previous owner of the Chicken Track deposited with the lawyer in

Chaparral Creek that started me off.'

'It's a good job she did leave it with the lawyer in view of what happened,' Purdom said. 'If there's anythin' in it, that is.'

'That document is sure gonna make some interestin' readin', one way or the other,' Kitchenbrand said.

'If we ever get that far,' the marshal added.

Conversation dwindled, and when they had finished their smokes and the last of the coffee was gone they settled down for the night. Kitchenbrand and Purdom agreed times to keep watch but they excused Garland from guard duties, despite his protests. He had no sooner laid his head down than he was asleep.

'He'll be fine by tomorrow,' Kitchenbrand said.

Purdom lay back, his head on his saddle, and watched the firelight cast flickering shadows across the walls of the cave. The last thing he was conscious of was the figure of Kitchenbrand hunched in the cave entrance.

He was awakened by someone gently tugging at his shoulder. Instinctively his hand reached for the six-gun which was concealed beneath his blanket, but as his eyes grew used to the dim light he could see that it was Kitchenbrand. He put a finger to his mouth and signalled for Purdom to follow him. Purdom shook off his blankets and moved quickly to the mouth of the cave.

'Over there,' Kitchenbrand whispered.

Purdom's eyes followed Kitchenbrand's outstretched finger. Advancing down the river trail that they had followed was a group of riders. It was difficult to make out any details in the darkness but there seemed to be at least nine of them bunched together, with another two riding slightly behind.

'Seems like we weren't the only ones to find Garland,' Kitchenbrand said.

'Maybe they'll pass on by.'

'I doubt it. It won't be Garland's tracks they've followed, but ours. They might even have caught a slight glow from the embers of the fire.'

Purdom weighed up the situation. 'What do you think?' he asked. 'Do we stay here and fight or make a run for it?'

'Neither,' Kitchenbrand said. He glanced at Purdom's puzzled features. 'I don't like bein' bottled up. We move out of here but we don't run for it. We choose where we make a stand.'

Purdom grinned. 'I'd best rouse Garland,' he said.

It only took a moment to apprise Garland of what was happening, and not much longer for the three of them to slip out of the cave entrance and slide silently down the slope to where the horses were tied in the trees. Kitchenbrand reached forward and took a rifle from its scabbard.

'Here, take this,' he said to Garland. 'You're gonna need it.'

They didn't mount but led the horses, following the line of the hill away from where Kitchenbrand had seen the riders. The line of the trees gave them cover. After walking a short distance, they came to a spot where a winding trail seemed to lead up the side of the hill, which was not steep at this point.

'We'll take the trail,' Kitchenbrand said, 'and get above the varmints.'

'You figure they'll follow us?' Garland said.

'Ain't no doubt, and they won't be far behind neither.'

They climbed the hillside, following the trail which led upwards to a wide ledge and then on to another shelf where some boulders and bushes provided basic cover.

'This will do,' Kitchenbrand said. 'We'll take up position here. When they arrive at the first ledge they'll be exposed. That'll give us a decent chance.'

'I reckon it's as good a spot as any,' Purdom replied.

'Maybe we should keep movin'?' Garland said.

Kitchenbrand looked at him. Despite

the few hours of sleep he had managed to snatch, he still looked tired and worn. Kitchenbrand's rifle hung loosely in his hands.

'No point in goin' any further,' Kitchenbrand said. 'It would only be a matter of time till they caught up with us, them or some more of their cronies.'

'You figure there'll be others?' Purdom said.

'They'll be lookin' for Garland. And if they ain't, once they get sight of that burnt-out roost they're gonna be lookin' for us.'

Kitchenbrand led the horses away to a concealed spot where he could tether them. When he came back the others had taken their places behind the rocks. Kitchenbrand swung in alongside them.

'Can't be too long till they get here,' he said.

The sky was lightening with the approach of dawn. The last stars faded and from somewhere below them a bird began to sing in the treetops.

'Hope that ain't Reba,' Kitchenbrand said.

'Reba?' Purdom queried.

'It don't matter. Don't sound much like her.'

Garland said nothing and Kitchenbrand didn't know whether or not the boy knew what he was talking about. Kitchenbrand thought of the old woman. In a funny kind of way, he was missing her. He figured she would have relished the situation they were in. He wasn't so sure about the boy.

The minutes passed by. Daylight was flooding the landscape. They could see a good way down the trail before the angle of a hill cut off their view in that direction. Sounds carried quite far but Kitchenbrand could hear nothing. Could Addison and the Yuma boys have passed by after all? It had been finding the remains of the gunman who had fallen into the river that gave Kitchenbrand and the marshal the clue to finding Garland. They had figured out what might have happened and followed the river back, looking for any sign of the boy. They had seen the indications of where someone had crawled out of the water, but there had been an element of luck about it.

Maybe Addison wouldn't be lucky.

His thoughts were suddenly put to rest when he heard the jingle of harness. He glanced towards the others. Purdom had heard it too. Presently the neighing of a horse reached their ears and then the soft clump of horses' hoofs. Suddenly the early morning calm was riven by a series of loud bangs; bullets tore up the ground behind Kitchenbrand and shards of shattered rock went whining through the air.

Kitchenbrand rolled away from where he had been stationed and, lying on his side, squeezed the trigger of his Sharps rifle at two figures who were partly concealed in bushes higher up the mountain side. There was a scream and one of the men, flinging up his arms, came crashing down the hillside, hitting the ground with a loud thud just in front of Garland.

Kitchenbrand fired again, but the other man had ducked away. Another shot rang out from a little way to the right. Kitchenbrand couldn't be sure whether it was the same man or yet another, but either way it meant some of the Yuma boys had taken up a position above them.

'Cover me!' he shouted.

As both Purdom and Garland opened fire at the bushes on the hillside above, Kitchenbrand took to his heels and ran swiftly along the ledge, hurling himself behind another rock from which he could view the hillside from a different angle. As he had hoped, he had a clear side view of one of the outlaws. Taking aim, he fired and the man toppled backwards. There was a moment's stillness and then a haze of fire broke out from among the trees bordering the river.

Kitchenbrand cursed beneath his breath. He had been planning to catch the outlaws unawares, but he had not reckoned on any of them gaining the high ground. He had no way of knowing how many of them might still be up there, but even if there weren't any more the unavoidable exchange of fire had given warning to Addison and his men and given them the opportunity to take shelter. As if to corroborate his perception of the situation, a voice rang out from the direction of the trees.

'Is that you, Garland!'

Garland looked across at Kitchenbrand, who signalled for him to remain quiet. The voice came again, somewhat high-pitched and whiny. Kitchenbrand had heard the voice before. He was pretty sure it was Angel Addison.

'I know it's you, Garland!' There was a pause. When the voice called again, its appeal was not to Garland but to his companions.

'Whoever else is there, you ain't got a chance of escapin'. There's plenty of us and we got the place covered!' Again there was a pause before Addison continued: 'Whoever you are, we ain't got no quarrel with you. Just hand over Garland and you can ride free!'

Kitchenbrand looked up at the hillside. Was there anyone else up there? His keen eyes could detect no sign of movement. If he could get higher, he could edge his way along the hillside and get into a position where he might be able to see Addison and open up a new front. He was unconsciously thinking in terms of the Civil War. Another question he needed to take into account was how much Addison could see of the bench on which they had taken their position. Judging from the waywardness of his group's shooting, probably not very much.

There was one way of putting it to the test, and that was by making his way back to Purdom and Garland. There was also still the possibility of a sniper being positioned above. Without thinking any further, Kitchenbrand got to his feet and, bent double, quickly made his way back to his original hiding-place.

'What are you doin?' Purdom said. 'You were takin' some risk.'

Quickly, Kitchenbrand explained his intentions to the others.

'I'm not sure I like it,' Purdom said. 'Maybe we should all try and get up the hill.'

Kitchenbrand shook his head. 'Too big a risk of being seen if we all go for it.'

'At least take Garland. I can hold things here.'

Kitchenbrand looked at the youngster. 'There ain't time to argue,' he said. 'Just make sure you keep out of sight.' He turned back to Purdom. 'You can do more than hold things,' he said. 'Wait till me and Garland get into position. When we have, I'll fire a shot. When you hear it, start shootin'.'

'I get you,' Purdom said. 'You're figurin' you'll be able to locate 'em that way.'

Kitchenbrand winked. 'You and me think alike,' he said. 'Just be careful you don't take any chances when they start firin' back.'

With a nod to Purdom, Kitchenbrand began to climb the hillside. It wasn't difficult and there was sufficient cover for concealment even if Addison's view of things wasn't obscured by his angle of vision. Kitchenbrand reached the level from which the gunnies had fired down on them. The second man's corpse lay stretched out at a little distance to his right. There were no indications of anyone else. He glanced down to see the figure of Garland coming up behind him. There seemed to be only a further short climb to the top of the hill and he started again. When he reached what, appeared to be the summit it proved to be a wide pasture which extended further back to where the slope continued. It didn't matter. He reached down a hand to haul Garland up the rest of the way.

'Follow me,' he said, 'but stay back from the edge and don't get skylined.' There had been a break in proceedings but now the voice of Addison rang out again.

'You hear what I said? We ain't got no quarrel with anyone but Garland. Just send him out and you can ride away. I'll give you five minutes to make your mind up. After that we're comin' to get him!'

Kitchenbrand glanced at Garland, then continued moving. He was less concerned about whether Addison would be able to see them than he was that there might be more of the outlaws along the hill. As he moved he kept on the alert. The section they were moving along began to run out as a shoulder of the hill came down in a line of trees.

'No point in goin' any further,' he said.

He lay down on the grass and took a good look around. To his disappointment, he could not see the outlaws. 'It was just a chance,' he said to Garland. 'It woulda been a big help, but it ain't necessary. Get ready, because once I give Purdom the signal and they start shootin', that'll be our chance.'

Garland nodded. Once they were both happy that they had taken up suitable positions, Kitchenbrand raised his six-gun and fired.

Almost instantaneously a burst of gunfire issued from the trees. Some of the bullets were aimed in Kitchenbrand's direction but most of the fire was concentrated on the side of the hill where Purdom remained. Kitchenbrand was confident that there was little chance of it troubling him, but he and Garland had a clear indication now of where the outlaws were situated. They both began to pump lead.

A fresh crescendo of gunfire burst from the trees, more of it aimed this time at the hillside where Kitchenbrand and Garland were situated. There was a disturbance in the underbrush and for a few moments Kitchenbrand had a clear sight of some of the outlaws. He continued firing. Garland had used all his ammunition and was jamming fresh shells into his weapon. When he had done so he placed the rifle against his shoulder and commenced firing again. Streamers of smoke now indicated where the gunnies were concealed and Kitchenbrand was pretty sure that his tactic had them confused.

'They might think we've been joined by reinforcements,' he commented. 'They can't be too comfortable about bein' fired on from two positions.'

Firing ceased and in the lull Kitchenbrand half-expected to hear Addison's voice calling to them again, but there was no repetition. A fresh burst of shooting came from along the hillside and Kitchenbrand grinned.

'Purdom is still doin' his best to pick them off,' he said. He looked across at Garland. The boy had a grin on his face too. Any doubts Kitchenbrand might have had about his readiness for the fight had been put at rest. He had acquitted himself like Virginy's grandson.

The comparative quiet continued. Kitchenbrand was feeling a little puzzled till a new sound broke on his ears; the neighing of a horse. The sound was repeated, followed by the thud of horses' hoofs. Garland threw Kitchenbrand a puzzled look.

'They've had enough for now,' Kitchenbrand said. 'They've gone back and taken to their horses.'

The sound of movement was unmistakable and then Kitchenbrand caught a glimpse of riders through the trees. He raised his rifle and loosed off a couple of shots, but the riders were too far away and screened by the trees. Kitchenbrand and Garland stood up and watched the riverbank. Presently the riders appeared, moving away at a steady pace.

'How many?' Kitchenbrand called.

'I see eight of 'em,' Garland said.

'Yeah. I wonder how many they left behind?'

They watched the retreating riders for a few moments before starting back to where they had left Purdom. The marshal had lit a cigarette and was

175

leaning against the rock with his rifle at his side.

'Looks like your little ruse worked, Kitchenbrand,' he said, tossing his tobacco pouch in their direction.

'Maybe not quite as I anticipated,' Kitchenbrand replied, 'but good enough to get us out of a tight situation.'

'I figure we got an extra advantage, and that is they can't be sure how many of us there are. When Addison started callin', he probably figured that there were not more than two or three of us. Because of the way your plan worked out, he probably figures there's more of us now.'

'That's the way we figured it,' Garland said.

'How are you feelin'?' Kitchenbrand said to him.

'Hell, I'm feelin' fine now. Funny what a little gunplay can do. Guess I was just sick of bein' on the receivin' end.'

'Well,' Kitchenbrand said, 'It ain't

over yet. Not by a long way. Addison is goin' to link up with the rest of his men and he's gonna come lookin' for us again.'

'Let 'em come,' Garland said. 'Just so long as I got a fightin' chance.'

They sat back and enjoyed their smokes. Then Kitchenbrand stood up. 'I believe we were settin' out for Addison's roost to pick up a horse,' he said.

'Won't that be a mite more dangerous now?' Purdom said. 'There's a pretty good chance those varmints will head back there to regroup.'

'They're gonna get quite a surprise!' Garland said. They all laughed.

'They sure are!' Kitchenbrand replied. He looked out over the scene and laughed again. 'Well, looks like we don't need to,' he said. 'Take a look by those trees.'

Purdom and Garland looked in the direction he indicated. Just emerging form the vegetation was a brown horse.

'Must have belonged to one of the

outlaws we shot,' Kitchenbrand said. 'Now wasn't that nice of 'em? He's all saddled and ready to go.'

'Just one question,' Purdom said. 'If we ain't goin' near Addison's hideout, or what's left of it — '

'And that's nothin'!' Garland interrupted.

'Like I say, if we ain't goin' by the ashes, just where are we goin'?'

The three of them looked at each other. After the successful outcome of the battle they were all on a high and they broke into laughter again.

'Hell,' Kitchenbrand said. 'I guess I oughta give it some thought!'

6

Angel Addison surveyed the ruins of his outlaw roost. His initial outburst of rage had subsided to be replaced by a burning lust for revenge. He paced up and down beside the burnt-out ashes of his cabin, dashing his fist into his other hand at regular intervals.

'Who the hell could have done this?' he shouted.

The Yuma boys were stilled. Nobody attempted to reply, not even his right-hand man Cord. They had seen Addison in a rage before, but never like this.

'That dirty stinkin' skunk Garland is gonna pay,' he yelled. 'He's got to be involved in this somehow.'

Most of his listeners were conscious that he was ranting. They knew enough to know that Garland could not have had anything to do with it.

'Has anybody seen Delta Trace?' Addison fumed. 'Where in hell has she gone?'

His befuddled brain sought desperately for a culprit. In his state of mind, anyone would do. His anger burned him with a brand of unreasoning hate, but through the fumes and fog in his brain an insistent thought began to drum. Landon Clovis. Could he be involved somehow? He had made an arrangement to meet Clovis and bring Garland. That wasn't going to happen now. Clovis had expressed some disapproval and distaste of the Yuma gang. Clovis had been irritating him for some time.

Then a dim memory began to stir. What was it Clovis had said about Garland's grandmother? That she had been seen riding with some stranger? And what about the marshal they had shot in the course of abducting Garland? He had a personal motive for revenge quite apart from his role as a lawman. Could there be some sort of tie-in? And who could the stranger be?

His confused brain reeled. He needed to cut through it all. The likeliest place Garland and whoever was with him would head for would be Chaparral Bend. That was the obvious place to go. Chaparral Bend was close to the Latigo spread. He would be right on hand to deal with Clovis if that became necessary.

He looked at the circle of desperados around him. They were waiting for a word from him, a word that would release the tension that had built up in them.

'OK. Let's go get the stinkin' varmints who did this!' he yelled.

There was answering roar; shots were fired into the air. The Yuma boys were on their way and someone was going to pay. And it really didn't matter who.

* * *

Kitchenbrand's first inclination had been to head for Chaparral Bend without any delay, but on further consideration he wasn't so sure.

'I gotta get back there pretty soon,' Purdom said. 'I trust my deputy to do a job. Bert Hardy is a good man but I don't like to leave things too long.'

'Yeah, of course,' Kitchenbrand replied, 'but think about it for a moment. When Addison and his boys get themselves organized, what are they goin' to do?'

'They're gonna come lookin' for us,' Garland replied.

'Yes. And they'll figure we'll head straight back for Chaparral Bend.'

'I see what you mean,' Purdom said.

'So what do we do? Stay here in the hills?' Garland interposed.

'When they see what we did to their hideout,' Purdom said, 'they ain't gonna leave any of their other haunts unprotected.'

'Addisonville was their main hole in the wall. They're gonna be so mad they won't think of nothin' except findin' us.'

They had ridden a little way along the river, following the trail by which Kitchenbrand and Purdom had arrived at the river, and were sitting their horses in the shelter of some trees. As they spoke, their eyes searched the terrain for the presence of outlaws. Garland leaned forward and stroked his horse's mane. He was thinking back, trying to recall something Addison had said when he and his men had come to get him from the room in which he had been held captive.

'I just remembered somethin',' he said. 'Somethin' Addison let slip. When one of his men was beatin' me up, he told him to stop after a while because Clovis would want me in one piece.'

Kitchenbrand and Purdom looked at each other. Garland's words were a confirmation of what they had felt all along: that Clovis was deeply involved.

'Did he say anythin' else?' Kitchenbrand snapped.

Garland shook his head. 'No, I don't

think so. I tried to get more information out of Addison when we were ridin' along, just before I took that plunge into the river, but he didn't say anythin' more.'

Kitchenbrand's brows were puckered. When he spoke again he was voicing the others' thoughts too.

'It looks like Addison was takin' you to see Clovis. OK. Why not let the meetin' take place? It would give us an entry to the Latigo and might just help make everythin' a lot clearer.'

'And you two pass as members of the Yuma gang?' Garland asked.

Purdom shook his head. 'That wouldn't work,' he said. 'Clovis knows me.'

Kitchenbrand scratched his chin, continuing to think about the problem. 'Hell,' he concluded, 'we can think about that one as we ride.'

'If Addison gets back to Clovis first, we could all be ridin' into a death trap,' the marshal said.

Kitchenbrand grinned. 'Seems like

we been doin' plenty of that already,' he said. 'And we're still alive and kickin'.'

*   *   *

As Addison rode hard with his gang towards Chaparral Bend, he began to calm down a little. As they approached a stand of trees set back from the main trail, he drew the band to a halt.

'What is it?' Cord asked.

'Where do you think Garland and his friends are right now?' Addison said.

Cord shrugged his shoulders. 'Could be either ahead of us or behind us.'

'I figure they're behind us. Apart from anythin' else, they don't know the country like we do. They'll be goin' slow, on the lookout for us. So why don't we set a little trap for 'em?'

'There's plenty of us. Guess we could spare a few men.'

'That's what I was thinkin'. If Garland is ahead of us, it's no skin off our noses.' He rose in the saddle.

'Rogan! Newsome! Get over here.' He turned back to Cord. 'Take those two and find a position among those cottonwoods where you won't be seen and wait to see if Garland comes by.'

'He might not ride this way.'

'That's not likely. Anyone heading in the direction of Chaparral Bend is almost certain to follow this trail.'

Cord nodded. 'Leave it to us,' he said. 'How long do you figure we should give it?'

'Wait till about this time tomorrow. You can set up camp tonight, make yourselves comfortable. Here, just in case there are more of them than we figure, you can take Smith and Hordern too.'

'That won't be necessary,' Cord replied with a leer. 'If Garland comes down that trail, he's gonna be a sittin' duck. Same goes for anyone riding with him. They won't know what hit 'em.'

'I'm tempted to stay behind myself,' Addison said with a grin, 'but I got business in Chaparral Bend. We'll see you there.'

* * *

Kitchenbrand, Purdom and Garland rode at an easy pace, not wanting to tire their horses. They had made their way out of the hills without seeing anyone. From time to time one or the other of them looked back but there was no sign of pursuit. Then, after riding further, they came across the sign left by Addison and his party and there was no need to check on their back trail. They dismounted to take a closer look.

'Couldn't be more obvious,' Kitchenbrand said.

'I'd say about fifteen or more of 'em,' Garland added.

They rode on, confident in the knowledge that Addison was ahead. Kitchenbrand had been racking his brains about what to do when they got near Clovis's Latigo spread. At least

Addison's trail would give him some indication of what the outlaw and his gang were likely to be doing.

★ ★ ★

Even before riding to the Buzzards with Kitchenbrand, Virginy had been familiar with most of the terrain around Chaparral Bend, and she and Delta made good progress. The land was gently rolling with occasional stands of trees, and deserted, so it came as a surprise when Virginy noticed a smudge of dust on the skyline off to their right.

'Unless I'm mistaken, that dust is bein' kicked up by a bunch of horses.'

'You mean there are some riders coming towards us?'

'They're a good ways off yet,' Virginy replied. 'All the same, I figure it might be sensible for us to take cover.'

Digging her heels into her horse's flanks, she led the way off the trail in the direction of some tall cottonwoods. They rode into the trees, then drew their mounts to a halt. The cotton-woods rustled and from their depths a crow cawed. Virginy turned to her companion.

'Now you don't suppose that could be Reba?' she said. The girl smiled and shook her head. She was aware that Virginy was joking in order to steady her, but the strange thing was that she didn't feel nervous. Since she had been rescued from the clutches of Angel Addison she felt a different person. She had recovered her old self.

'Whoever those riders are,' Virginy said, 'they ain't gonna find us here.'

She slid from the saddle and Delta followed her. After tying their horses they had started to move further into the trees when Virginy paused, went back to the horse and drew a rifle from its scabbard.

'Picked this up in Chaparral Bend,' she said. 'We'll wait here till those riders have gone. We're probably makin' somethin' out of nothin', but it don't hurt to be careful.'

They started to move forward once more when suddenly Virginy stopped and, turning to Delta, put her finger to her lips. They both froze. Virginy pointed ahead. They listened but all they could hear was the breeze whispering in the trees. Then they both heard something else — a faint murmur of voices.

'There's someone up ahead,' Virginy whispered.

'What do we do, go back?' the girl asked.

Virginy thought for a moment. 'I'd like to know just who it is. You wait here. I'll carry on and try taking a look.'

The girl shook her head. 'I'm coming with you,' she said.

Virginy didn't argue. Together, they crept forward. Although they listened intently, they could no longer hear any voices. Delta was beginning to think that they must have been mistaken when there was another sound; the unmistakable snicker of horses.

Again Virginy put her finger to her lips. The trees were thinning and Virginy could tell that they were approaching an edge of the wooded patch more or less on the side furthest away from where they had entered. Peering ahead, she suddenly thought she detected movement. Then her eyes travelled downwards and she saw some figures lying in the grass near the trees. One of them suddenly stood up and Virginy could tell that the girl had seen him too, because she started involuntarily.

'I know that man,' she said. 'He's called Cord. He's one of Addison's men.'

'The Yuma boys,' Virginy said. She motioned to the girl to move back. When they had retraced their steps a little way they stopped and took cover.

'Are you sure you recognized that man?' Virginy asked.

'Yes. I'd know him anywhere.'

Virginy looked puzzled. 'I'd like to know what they're doin' in the woods.'

Suddenly a light of understanding dawned in her eyes. 'I reckon they're waitin' for someone,' she said. 'And if they're the Yuma boys, they ain't doin' it to be friendly.'

'What? You think they're waitin' to ambush someone?'

'Yes. Where they're camped, they've got a clear view of the trail.' Her mouth opened a little wider. 'Kitchenbrand!' she said. 'I bet they're waitin' for Kitchenbrand and the marshal. I wonder how long they've been here?' She thought for a moment longer and then touched Delta's arm. 'You get on back to where we left the horses,' she said.

'What are you gonna do?'

'I'm goin' to stick around and see what happens. I got a feelin' I might be needed.'

'And I got a feelin' we might both be needed,' Delta replied. She reached into her skirt and produced a Colt Army revolver.

'You aren't the only one can handle a

gun,' she said. 'I'm stickin' with you.'

Virginy was about to argue but, seeing the determined look on the girl's face, she did not attempt to dissuade her. After all, it was good that Delta believed in herself again.

'Don't make any noise,' Virginy said. 'And keep that gun out of sight.'

Delta smiled and they began to move forward again to where they had a view of the owlhoots. They could see now that there were three of them. Concealing themselves in the undergrowth, the two women began to watch.

They didn't have long to wait. Suddenly the outlaws became animated and jumped to their feet. They began talking to one another but neither Virginy nor Delta could make out the words. They didn't need to, however, because it was apparent what the gunnies were about. They slid away from the patch of comparatively open ground where they had been lying to take up position behind some trees. Virginy had a shrewd guess that whoever they were waiting for was fast approaching.

From what she could see, the outlaws had chosen their hiding-places well. The trees behind which they were concealed were on the edge of the woods and the site commanded a good view of the trail. She glanced at Delta. The girl signalled that she was OK. Virginy shifted her position slightly. She couldn't see anything but soon her ears caught the sound of horses. She was thinking rapidly, trying to decide on the best course of action. If it was Kitchenbrand coming down the trail, the best thing would be to fire a shot in warning. If it wasn't, she would be giving her position away. But what if the approaching riders were more of Addison's gang?

She leaned forward, her eyes straining to catch a glimpse of who the newcomers might be. Then her heart skipped. She couldn't be certain of who the other two riders were, but her old eyes could not mistake the sight of her grandson. Her sight was good and she would know him anywhere.

Without further hesitation, she raised her rifle and was about to fire a warning shot when she saw one of the outlaws raise his gun. Instantly she brought her rifle down and, steadying herself for a moment, aimed and fired. The rifle boomed and she felt the recoil slam against her shoulder. Almost in the same instant the man opened fire on the approaching riders but Virginy's bullet caught him in the shoulder and he fell forward, his shot slamming harmlessly into the ground.

Immediately there came a fusillade of shooting from various directions. Out of the corner of her eye Virginy saw a stab of flame. Delta had fired her weapon. Virginy aimed and fired again; she saw a branch of a tree fall to the ground. Then a bullet thudded into a tree next to her and she realized that she was under attack.

Shouting to Delta, she began to run back through the trees. Both of them kept running till they found cover behind more trees and stopped to look back. Gunfire was ringing out but there didn't seem to be any sign of pursuit and no bullets came their way.

'I guess that warnin' shot musta worked,' Virginy said. 'Those varmints have got their hands full now fighting off Ty and the others.'

'Ty!' Delta gasped.

'Yes. One of those riders was Ty and I guess the other two are Kitchenbrand and the marshal.'

Delta's smile was radiant as she reached out to hug the old lady.

'Jumpin Jehosophat!' Virginy said. 'Just be careful that gun don't go off.'

The sounds of firing grew more insistent, then suddenly there was silence. The two women exchanged glances.

'What do you think's happened?' Delta asked.

'Well,' Virginy replied, 'seems like one side or the other has won out.' They looked at each other again, afraid of what might have happened.

'Come on,' Virginy said, 'there's only one way to find out.'

Holding their guns in readiness, they crept forward once more. When they got to the spot from which they had originally viewed the outlaws, they paused. They were near the edge of the woods and going further would place them in an exposed position. They both peered ahead, trying to see what had become of the gunhawks. There was no sign of any of them. Then they heard the sound of voices. Virginy raised her rifle in readiness. The voices got closer and a figure came into view. It was Kitchenbrand. He was bent double, glancing to right and left before running forward to hurl himself behind the cover of a tree. He was looking towards them but had not seen anything. Virginy dropped her rifle and called out.

'Kitchenbrand, it's Virginy, Virginy Garland! And I got Delta here with me!'

Kitchenbrand emerged from behind the tree, his rifle still at the ready.

'Virginy!' he shouted, and his tone of voice indicated his amazement.

The old lady nodded to the girl and they both stepped from concealment. At the same moment Virginy saw the marshal coming up behind Kitchenbrand and, just behind him, her longed-for grandson.

'I can't believe it,' she muttered. Ty began to run and the next thing Virginy was aware of was being held in his arms. Kitchenbrand and the marshal waited a few moments before coming forward.

'Landogoshen!' Virginy murmured at last. 'Is this really happenin'?'

'Seems like we owe you our lives, ma'am,' the marshal said. 'We sure feel grateful.'

When his joy and relief at seeing his grandmother had calmed, Ty held her at arm's length. 'You always stood by me,' he said.

Virginy looked to Kitchenbrand. 'You

got this man to thank for savin' you from the noose,' she said. 'Him and the marshal both.'

'I know,' Ty said. 'They done a lot more for me too.' He seemed to become aware of the girl for the first time. Virginy, perceiving that Delta had been to some extent ignored, introduced her to her grandson. He hesitated for a moment and then awkwardly removed his hat.

'Glad to make your acquaintance,' he mumbled. Kitchenbrand, observing that the young man seemed to have become suddenly tongue-tied, turned to Virginy and began an explanation of what had happened. While he was doing so Purdom moved away to check on the condition of the outlaws. All three were dead.

The marshal reflected upon how easily their roles might have been reversed; on how close he, Kitchenbrand and Garland had come to being in the outlaws' shoes. It was true what Kitchenbrand had said. Virginy Garland was quite a lady.

Angel Addison, with the rest of his gang, drew rein outside the ranch house of the Latigo spread. He sat for a moment looking about.

'Where is everyone?' he said.

'We didn't see nobody as we were ridin' in here,' one of his men replied.

'Go and take a look inside the bunkhouse.'

The man urged his horse forward. Coming to a halt, he slid from the saddle and disappeared inside. After a few moments he reappeared.

'Nobody there!' he shouted.

Addison's teeth were gritted. 'Now what do you suppose Clovis is up to?' he said.

'Maybe he's out on the range somewhere. Maybe he's at that line shack you were supposed to be meetin' him at.'

Addison continued to sit mute and grim-faced. There was something about the quietness which unsettled him.

Something was not quite right. Suddenly, as if in answer to his questions, the door of the ranch house opened and Clovis appeared. At the same moment the shutters of the building flew wide and gun barrels were pushed through; men appeared on the roof of the ranch house and the adjoining buildings with rifles pointed at the little group of horsemen. Clovis stepped on to the veranda and behind him three men emerged, also carrying arms.

'Hello, Addison. I been expectin' you,' Clovis said.

Addison looked about him. A drop of sweat appeared on his forehead. 'Why the welcomin' committee?' he said.

'Let's just say we heard you were comin'. Since you didn't turn up with Garland, I figured somethin' must have gone wrong.'

'Garland got away but it won't take long till we round him up.'

'I'd say that was more than a little careless.' The rancher's tone annoyed

Addison. It didn't take much to grate on him.

'What are you doin' here?' Clovis said.

Addison had to think for a moment. 'You want Garland,' he said, 'and so do I. But I want whoever's been helpin' him even more.'

'Then it seems we're after pretty much the same thing,' Clovis replied. 'Now, it seems to me we ain't goin' about things the right way facin' each other in some kind of stand-off like this. I'd say it would make a lot more sense for us to pool our resources and go and get Garland and his friends. And since they're almost certain at some point to make an appearance in Chaparral Bend, that's the place we ought to be.'

'Some of my boys are in town already,' Addison said.

'That's fine. I'll leave a few of my men here to keep an eye on things and the rest of us will head out.' He turned to the man with the rifle standing next to him and issued a few instructions.

'Just give us a few minutes to get saddled up and we'll be right with you,' he added.

He turned on his heel and made for the stables, thinking rapidly. It had been his policy so far to dissociate himself from Addison, but there didn't seem to be much point in doing so any longer. He wouldn't be able to keep their acquaintance from public attention much longer. Already people like the marshal were aware of it. But the new situation provided him with an opportunity. A lot of the townsfolk were still angry with Garland. They still held him responsible for the bank robbery. If he played his cards right, he could get the information he wanted from Garland before doing his duty as a good citizen and handing him over to the law. There might yet be a use for that gallows. Furthermore, if things worked out, it would round things off nicely if Garland was to be joined by Angel Addison.

* * *

Deputy Marshal Bert Hardy was looking anxiously up and down the street and wishing the marshal was back. Chaparral Bend was not known as a rowdy place; Purdom had seen to that. But earlier that morning a bunch of riders had stormed into town and already things threatened to get out of hand. They had made themselves at home in the saloon and even at that hour and from a distance the noise they were making was shattering the peace. He could rely on a few of the townsfolk to back him up if matters got really bad, but he wasn't confident.

For the second time that day he made his way down the main drag towards the saloon. Just as he got near, the batwings flew open and a couple of men fell into his path, grappling with each other and rolling in the dust. As they struggled to their feet one of them landed a vicious kick in the other's groin. He doubled up but before his assailant could land another blow the deputy marshal had seized him by the arm. At the same moment a whistling, jeering crowd of spectators spilled out of the saloon, shouting and cursing. One of them drew his six-gun and began firing into the air.

'That's enough!' Hardy shouted. He was trying to hold the two fighters apart and deal with the crowd at the same time. A few people who had been out on the street moved rapidly away from the scene. The man with the gun spat into the dust.

'Now what's the problem, Deputy?' he hissed. He peered mockingly at Hardy. 'Ain't we seen you someplace before?' Some of his friends began to laugh. The deputy pushed the man he was holding to one side.

'I told you boys to take things easy,' he said. 'There's no need for more trouble. Just go back on in and leave me to handle things between these two.'

The man began to laugh. '*Leave me to handle things here*,' he mimicked. In an instant his expression changed and he swung the gun he had been firing into the air towards the deputy. Hardy was quicker. In an instant his own gun was spitting lead and the man reeled back, clutching his shoulder and dropping his gun into the dust. Hardy swung round to face the crowd of hardcases who had gathered on the boardwalk.

'OK, you heard what I said. Go back inside.'

For a moment the issue hung in the balance. The deputy licked his lips but otherwise gave no indication of the tension that had built up inside him. The men looked at one another and then at the injured man. Suddenly they broke and made for the batwings. Hardy waited till they had gone, then turned to the two who had been fighting. 'You either call it off and join your friends or you come with me to the jailhouse,' he said.

The man who had been kicked in the groin, now back on his feet, looked at his assailant with a murderous stare, but after a moment they both made their way back through the batwings. The man who had been shot in the shoulder made to do so but the deputy marshal stepped between him and the batwings.

'Not you,' he said. He bent down and picked up the man's gun. 'You ain't got a choice. You're comin' with me to the jailhouse.'

Pushing the man in front of him, the deputy made his way back to the marshal's office. When he had locked the door of the cell on his prisoner he returned to his desk, reached into a drawer and poured himself a drink. He took a deep draught, then blew out his cheeks in a sigh of relief. By force of will he had got away with it this time. But he knew the hardcases in the saloon had only just started. Sooner or later they would probably come looking for their comrade. Things were going to get tough. How many of the townsfolk could he really rely on when the chips were down? Now he came to think about it, the town was strangely quiet. Maybe people had detected a taste of something in the air, a hint of menace.

Time passed. He took another few drinks, taking it slowly, and was considering whether to check things out again at the saloon when suddenly his ears picked up a sound: the unmistakable rhythm of hoof beats. He got to his feet, moved to the door and flung it open. For a few moments he felt a surge of relief. Could it be the marshal and the stranger — what was his name; Kitchenbrand?

His sense of elation was quickly dashed. The sound of hoofs was too loud. There were too many riders. He looked along the main street and saw them coming. They came along at a steady pace and even before they had got close to him he recognized them as the same types he had been dealing with earlier. So it came as something of a surprise for him to see Landon Clovis, the owner of the Latigo, with a few men he recognized as Latigo cowhands, riding with them. They were a tough looking gang and as they rode by in a cloud of dust he had a feeling that whatever Clovis was doing with them, it was the Yuma boys he had to deal with.

★   ★   ★

Kitchenbrand couldn't help thinking that his little group made an oddly assembled party that rode the last few miles into Chaparral Bend. He had been thinking about Garland's suggestion that they should continue to the Latigo and pose as Addison's men, but he didn't like it. Apart from what the marshal had said, he couldn't see that there was a lot to be gained by it.

Whatever Clovis was after, it seemed to him that the answer lay in the document which the previous owner of the Chicken Track had deposited with the attorney in Chaparral Bend. The marshal was anxious to get back there, so there was another reason to head for town.

The only worry was what sort of reception they might get when they arrived. Some folk still held Garland responsible for the bank job. Quite apart from whatever Addison or Clovis might be up to, it was possible that they would get a hot reception from the townsfolk themselves. He had seen how easily they had been stirred up into forming a lynch mob. Would things have calmed down much since then?

As the first outlying adobe shacks hove into view, Kitchenbrand drew his horse to a halt and turned to Virginy.

'There's likely to be a heap of trouble once we get to town,' he said. 'I think you and Delta ought to head back to the cabin.'

Delta had drawn her horse up close behind and before Virginy could reply, she broke in herself.

'There's no way Virginy and I are leavin' now,' she said. 'Ain't that so, Virginy?'

The old lady gave a snaggle-toothed smile. 'That's the way I figure it,' she said.

Kitchenbrand pointed to the sign they were following, evidence that the Yuma gang had already passed that way. 'Looks like Addison could be ready and waitin'.'

Delta looked suddenly grim. 'Addison owes me,' she said. 'I ain't likely to forget what he done to me. He's got to pay.'

Kitchenbrand looked towards the marshal for support but Purdom just shrugged. Garland tried to expostulate. 'Kitchenbrand's right,' he said. 'This ain't no show for a lady.'

'Are you includin' me in that description?' Virginy cackled.

Garland blushed. 'I was thinkin' more . . . ' he began, but puttered to a halt.

'There's no use in arguin',' Delta said. 'I've got as big a stake in all this as any of you, maybe more of one. I was never afraid, leastways not till Addison brought me low. That's all changed now. I ain't never goin' to be that way again.'

Kitchenbrand gave her a searching look, then reached for a rifle.

'Here,' he said, 'that six-shooter you got is fine, but you might need this too.'

Delta took it. 'Come on,' she said, 'we're wastin' time here. We got business to attend to.'

* * *

Deputy Marshal Hardy got to his feet and moved to the window. He had heard some sounds coming from outside but it was more of a feeling he had that something was happening. Sure enough, a group of men were walking towards the marshal's office, among whom he recognized a few of the Yuma boys who had been drinking in the saloon. He reached out and grabbed his rifle, which was leaning against the wall behind his chair, opened the door and stepped on the boardwalk. He had been wondering how long his bluff would last. Now he had the answer. A couple of the men were staggering and he realized that they were all the worse for drinking. As they came closer he raised his rifle.

'That's far enough,' he rasped.

The man who appeared to be their leader was a mean-looking *hombre* with a drooping moustache and a badly scarred face.

'We've come to get Fosdyke,' he replied.

'If you mean the man I placed under arrest for brawling in the street, he'll get a fair hearing when the judge is next in town.'

'We ain't waitin' for no judge.'

The man raised his hand to his mouth to form a sort of trumpet and suddenly began to bellow: 'Fosdyke, we come to set you free.'

From inside the building a voice hallooed in reply: 'Is that you, Turnbull? I knowed you'd come.'

'I figure you'd better turn him loose,' Turnbull said.

Something caught the marshal's eye and he glanced up the street. Another group of men was walking towards him. As they moved, some of them began to spread out and take up positions as if they were expecting some new arrival. Turnbull and the rest of the desperadoes turned to observe what was happening too. A broad grin spread across the gunman's face.

'Here comes Addison,' he said to the man standing next to him. He turned back to Hardy.

'You know who that is?' he said. 'That's Angel Addison. Maybe you've heard of him.' The deputy marshal tried not to let his features betray any of the emotion he was feeling. 'Angel ain't gonna like this one little bit. He don't take kindly to one of his men bein' put in jail.'

Hardy switched his attention to the approaching outlaw. He looked like a boy but he had heard of his reputation.

At least his arrival had given him a few more minutes.

'What's goin' on, Turnbull?' Addison said. He gave Hardy a disdainful glance.

'The deputy here got Fosdyke in jail.'

'What are you doin'?' Fosdyke's voice called. 'Come on, boys, get me outa here. What are you waitin' for?'

Addison's upper lip curled. 'Seems to me like you better set him loose, Deputy,' he snarled.

'He's under arrest. If you've got any authority over these men, I suggest you tell them go back to the saloon.'

Addison's face broke into the twisted semblance of a laugh.

'You hear that?' he said to the assembled gang. 'He suggests I tell you to go back to the saloon.' There was an outburst of laughter. Hardy's hand tightened on the stock of his rifle. He was aware of sweat pouring down the neck of his shirt. The laughter of the gunhawks was followed by a strange and pregnant silence, which was suddenly broken by another voice which cut through the atmosphere like a cold knife:

'Addison, I got you right in my sights. Now do what the deputy says.'

Hardy and Addison exchanged glances. Addison raised his eyes. Standing on the roof of the building opposite with his rifle trained on him was a figure outlined against the sky. It was Kitchenbrand. At the moment Addison saw him, Turnbull's hand suddenly dropped to his side. Before his gun was in his hand, Kitchenbrand's rifle boomed and Turnbull crumpled, clutching at his arm as his gun clattered to the ground.

'Better tell your men not to try anything stupid!' Kitchenbrand shouted. 'If anyone does, the next bullet's for you.'

Hardy turned his attention from the figure of Kitchenbrand to that of Addison; the man's face was a mask of hate. Taking advantage of the situation, the deputy swung his rifle up. 'The rest of you had better move!' he snapped.

The other desperadoes stood indecisively. One of the men who had been lurching across the street began to mutter something incomprehensible. Turnbull was crouched on one knee, trying to stem the flow of blood from his injured arm. For what seemed a long time but was in fact only an instant the scene impressed itself on the deputy's brain with an unwonted sharpness and clarity; then the picture was broken into by the voice of Kitchenbrand calling out once more.

'Addison, it's Hollis Kitchenbrand. Take a good look. You remember me? I'm the man who put you inside the Yuma penitentiary!'

Hardy took a look at Addison's face. It was twisted in a fury of rage.

'Addison, I'm comin' down. This is between you and me. Have you got the guts to face me man to man?'

Addison spun round to face his tormentor. He was beside himself with anger.

'So it was you tore my place down!'

he yelled. 'I shoulda guessed. You're an old man, Kitchenbrand. You shoulda known better than to get mixed up in any of this.'

'I got plenty of back-up,' Kitchen-brand lied. 'Just in case any of your boys decide to get edgy.'

Addison licked his lips. He was pretty sure that Kitchenbrand was bluffing, but he couldn't be sure. He had seemed to have a few supporters back there in the fighting at the cave. He was caught in a quandary. He glanced round and saw the eyes of his men on him. The rage which was boiling inside him surged up like a fountain.

'I'm waitin' for you, Kitchenbrand,' he screamed.

Hardy's rifle was covering the gun-nies. They began to fan out as Addison stepped into the middle of the street. Some of them began to walk away. Hardy looked down the line of buildings. After a few moments of waiting Kitchenbrand stepped through the doorway. Slowly, he moved away from the boardwalk into the dusty street. He was aware of the risk he was taking.

Behind him more of the gunslicks were spilling out of the saloon. There was nothing to stop any of them taking a shot at him except what he had shouted to Addison about having back-up and the fact that Hardy had Addison covered. There was nothing else he could do about that aspect of the situation and he needed to concentrate all his attention on Addison.

Blocking everything else from his mind, he began to walk steadily forward. Addison remained standing. The sun was behind him and Kitchenbrand realized that that put him at a disadvantage. His eyes tightened. A strange stillness seemed to have descended on the town. Any townsfolk who had been on the streets had taken shelter. The little group of outlaws outside the marshal's office had stepped well away, leaving Addison exposed. He remained stationary, slightly crouched, his arms held out and his hands close to his holsters. He was large and dominant in Kitchenbrand's vision.

As Kitchenbrand drew steadily closer every peripheral object was blotted from his sight. He felt the old familiar calm take possession of him as his gaze focused on Addison, watching for the slightest indication of movement on the part of his opponent. The outlaw was carrying two guns. Kitchenbrand carried only one, worn on his left hip, butt foremost. He had got into the habit of wearing it that way from the days when he spent most of his time in the saddle, but practice had compensated for the slightly slower time a crossdraw usually required. He was close enough now to see the colour of Addison's eyes but he wasn't looking at them. Some men would watch for any sudden flicker of movement in an opponent's expression but Kitchenbrand didn't operate that way. He continued to concentrate on Addison's hands. The right hand hung slightly lower. Kitchenbrand knew from experience that Addison was right-handed. The right-hand gun was likely to be the favoured one. He drew to a halt.

'So we meet again Addison,' he said.

A nerve twitched in Addison's cheek. Suddenly two shots rang out in quick succession. Kitchenbrand felt a sharp pain in his thigh. At the same moment Addison's hand fell to his side. In an instant his gun was in his hand and spitting lead, but, quick as he was, Kitchenbrand was quicker. Their two guns went off almost simultaneously but it was Addison who staggered back as Kitchenbrand's bullet took him in the shoulder. If it hadn't been for the impact of the slug in his thigh, Kitchenbrand wouldn't have needed to take a second shot.

Addison's gun exploded again and Kitchenbrand felt the bullet whistle by his head. Taking a fraction of a second to steady himself, he squeezed the trigger of his Colt once more. This time

Addison didn't move. Kitchenbrand thought for a moment that he must have missed but when the smoke cleared and he saw the blank look in Addison's eyes, he knew otherwise. Addison stood upright but he was not seeing Kitchenbrand any more. He was not seeing anything. For a few more seconds he remained upright, then he fell forward, hitting the ground with a dull thud, where he lay lifeless, his blood oozing into the dirt.

Silence filled the street, but only for a fraction of time and then everything disintegrated in a cacophony of noise and a bustle of movement precipitated by gunfire which rang out from further down the drag. Instinctively Kitchenbrand turned and hobbled to the shelter of a doorway. The deputy dived for cover behind the partly opened door of the marshal's office as bullets smacked into the wall above his head. They both began pumping bullets in the direction of the saloon and its adjoining buildings, from which a fusillade of fire was pounding.

Kitchenbrand glanced across the street and up at the roof of one of the buildings; he was rewarded by a brief glimpse of Marshal Purdom firing down from his vantage point on the roof of the livery stables. Gunfire was also coining from lower down the street where Garland was in position with his grandmother and Delta. Kitchenbrand had reckoned they would be less exposed there. He wasn't worried about Virginy but the girl had too much to lose.

He looked back in the direction of the saloon. A few of the gunslicks had taken cover behind various objects but most of them seemed to have retreated back inside. Shots were being fired from the neighbouring buildings, and some of them were getting uncomfortably close. Taking a quick decision, he shouted to the deputy marshal.

'Hardy, cover me!'

Without waiting for a response, Kitchenbrand got to his feet and, ignoring the pain in his leg, ran as quickly as he was able to the door behind which Hardy was positioned. He crashed through and, as Hardy followed, firing rapidly in the direction of the saloon, he slammed the door behind them. Hardy glanced at Kitchenbrand's leg.

'I'll be OK,' Kitchenbrand said. 'It looks worse than it is. It's only a flesh wound.'

'You're losin' blood,' Hardy replied. 'Here, let me tie somethin' round it to stem the flow.'

Kitchenbrand shook his head but Hardy had already started removing his necktie. In a few seconds he had fastened it round Kitchenbrand's leg in a rough tourniquet.

'You got Addison,' he said.

Kitchenbrand didn't reply. He went to the window and peered along the street.

'I figure those gunnies aren't gonna put up much of a fight,' he said. 'At least, not if we can get to them.'

'Most of 'em have been drinkin' in

the saloon,' Hardy said. 'They won't be in a fit state for a fight, especially when they realize what's happened to Addison.'

'We just need to get in a better position,' Kitchenbrand said. He looked about. The gunnie in the cell had resumed shouting, demanding to know what was going on.

'Come on,' Kitchenbrand rapped, 'we'll go out the back and make our way down the alley towards the saloon.'

They slipped past the cell where the prisoner was continuing to curse and ask questions in a loud voice. Once outside the back door they quickly made their way in the direction of the saloon, the sounds of shooting growing louder as they approached it. They reached a narrow alley leading back to the main street.

'I figure there's a couple of gunnies in position at the far end,' Kitchenbrand said.

'Pretty stupid of them not to have kept an eye on things here,' Hardy replied.

Kitchenbrand took a moment to

prepare, then hurled himself through the entrance to the alley. Barely had he started running when bullets began to whistle around him. He had the advantage, however; he could see a small group of outlaws outlined against the street behind. With both guns blazing he blasted his way down the alley, followed closely by the deputy. He saw two of the outlaws fall and the rest scatter as he emerged into the open. He continued running, taking up a position behind a water trough from which he concentrated his fire on the saloon. The deputy halted at the opening to the alley and began to blaze away too. Shots were being poured down on the saloon and its nearby buildings from the roof of the livery stable and Kitchenbrand was sure Purdom must still be there.

Suddenly there was a loud explosion and smoke billowed from the saloon. In a few moments ribbons of flame began to flicker out of the building like lizards' tongues, then the batwings flew open and a group of gunnies emerged, running for shelter in all directions. Some of them took the risk of untying their horses from the hitch rail and started riding away down the street. Kitchenbrand saw a couple of them tumble from their saddles and couldn't help grinning. Virginy and the girl were proving their worth.

More outlaws came out of hiding in other buildings and, jumping on their horses, started to ride in the opposite direction. Bullets had been pinging from the side of the water trough and hissing into the water but there was less shooting taking place. Instead, the sounds of gunfire seemed to be coming from further away, from the direction in which the latest bunch of outlaws had gone.

Looking that way, Kitchenbrand was startled to see them riding back again, firing over their shoulders. As they clattered by it became apparent that they were galloping away from a second group of riders who were coming up behind them. He was nonplussed till he heard the deputy shouting to him:

'Latigo riders!'

As they passed by he could see the brand on some of their horses. So it seemed that Clovis had finally decided that it was time to part company with the Yuma boys. He watched the riders disappear down the street. There was some sporadic firing, then, from various places of concealment, the last of the outlaws emerged with their hands in the air.

Kitchenbrand waited for a few moments and then got to his feet. He looked across at the deputy who had also stepped from cover. He took a stride into the open and then spun to one side as a shot rang out from further down the street. He heard a scream and, looking up, saw a man with a rifle as he lurched and then fell from the roof of a building opposite. He hit the floor and seemed to bounce before lying still.

Kitchenbrand swung round. His finger was closing on the trigger of his six-gun when he saw a familiar figure standing on the sidewalk. It was Virginy and cradled against her shoulder was a smoking rifle.

'Lords a' mercy!' she shouted. 'That was a close call.'

Behind her the figures of her grandson and Delta Trace came into view; the girl was holding on to Garland's arm. In less than a minute they were all together facing the cowering remnants of the outlaws.

'Reckon I'd better take these varmints into custody,' Purdom said. 'That jail is sure gonna be full tonight.'

Smoke drifted across the street. Bodies lay scattered about, sprawled in the dust and in the shadow of the gallows.

'I guess there ain't gonna be no more trouble from the Yuma boys,' Kitchenbrand said. He turned to Garland. 'You won't have no more to worry about from the townsfolk,' he said. 'Some of these varmints will testify that you had nothin' to do with robbin' the bank.'

Virginy looked up at the gallows tree.

'Those coyotes deserve to hang,' she said, 'but I never did like the idea of a necktie party. Seems to me the best thing would be to tear it right back down again.'

'I wouldn't disagree with that,' Kitchenbrand said. He turned to Purdom. 'I guess that just leaves Clovis. The Latigo boys might finally have turned things in our favour but Clovis has still got some questions to answer.'

* * *

It was a strange group who gathered in the offices of Hubert Cox, attorney at law, a few days later. Kitchenbrand, his thigh swathed in bandages, was there together with Marshal Purdom and his deputy. Old Virginy had put on a new calico dress for the occasion and with her hair drawn back in a tight bun, fully looked the part of a grand old lady. Ty Garland and Delta Trace sat side by side looking slightly sheepish and it was obvious to the most unobservant eye

230

that there was something between them. Strangest of all was the bowed figure of Landon Clovis.

'Well,' said the lawyer, 'I think that about ties things up.' In his hand he held a parchment which he proceeded to roll up, fasten with a ribbon and hand to Virginy Garland. 'Just as a precaution, I have a copy of that document in my safe and we are all witnesses to what it says.'

'Are you quite clear about this?' Kitchenbrand said to the deflated ranch owner. 'That document proves that the property known as the Chicken Track and belonging to Virginy Garland extends beyond its current boundaries to include a big part of your spread, the Latigo.' Clovis nodded. 'You were pretty sure about it all along, but you didn't know about the title deeds.'

'Is that why you were so keen to get hold of Ty Garland?' Purdom said. 'Or was there more to it?'

'Addison had me by the tail,' Clovis said. 'He coulda pinned that bank job on me. I made a mistake ever getting involved with him.'

'You certainly did,' the lawyer said. 'I think you've blown any chances you might have had of a political career.'

'You can thank your men that you ain't behind bars with what's left of the Yuma boys right now. You owe them,' Kitchenbrand said.

'And you better be sincere when you talk about makin' reparations to the citizens of Chaparral Bend for some of the skulduggery you been indulgin' in,' Purdom added. 'And although you weren't directly responsible, you can start with rebuilding Virginy's ranch house. You might not have broken any laws, strictly speakin', but I'll be watchin' you.'

'So there really was nothin' in that story about a lost gold mine somewhere on the Chicken Track?' Ty Garland said.

'You always had too much imagination,' Virginy replied. 'Still, I might just do some diggin'.' She gave a cluck of laughter. 'After all this excitement, what's an old lady to do to keep occupied?'

The others laughed too, with the exception of Clovis. When they had finished, Virginy turned to Kitchenbrand. 'We all owe you,' she said. 'I know you once said you were just passin' through, but I hope, after all that's happened, you're goin' to stick around.'

Kitchenbrand got to his feet and walked to the open window. He glanced up at the gallows tree overlooking the lawyer's office. It was about to be dismantled, but for the moment a bird seemed to have found a resting-place on its cross-beam. As Kitchenbrand watched it opened its beak and cawed. Virginy's mouth opened as she cackled.

'Looks like old Reba's backin' me up.'

Kitchenbrand's glance fell from the crow to the streets of the town. 'Then I guess I got to stay awhiles,' he replied. 'Those Yuma boys are one thing, but Reba is somethin' else altogether.'